I0822752

Angela J. Ford

Melody of Midnight

A Tower Knights Tale

Editing & Proofreading: The Fiction Fix

Cover Art: Natalie Bernard Art

Naked Hardcover: Cover Dungeon Rabbit

1

ZEKIEL

Shadows stretched over the withered vineyard, and a slice of pale moonlight peeked from behind a cloud before hiding its face again. I moved like a thief; ironic, as though I had something to hide when I was king.

Holding the gilded harp against my chest, I plucked a few strings and waited.

Movement from behind a tree alerted me of something's presence. A tall figure strode out, a glimmer of red hair catching in the dusky light.

"Oren." I bared my fangs.

"Zekiel," he echoed back, his own wickedly sharp teeth flashing in the low light. "Why the midnight meeting?"

"I come with a warning. You just returned, but it's not safe. You should take your wife and leave."

Oren frowned. "You're in some kind of trouble, aren't you? I can help." He lifted his pipe.

"Put that damned thing away," I hissed. "Who knows what undead beings you'll call forth to shatter my land."

Oren chuckled. "I control the song of the pipe."

I grimaced, because that hadn't always been the truth. Oren—whom I hadn't expected to see ever again —had suddenly reappeared in my realm: broken, married, and not quite his usual snarly self. As much as I appreciated being reunited with an old friend, I was also a king, and it was my duty to protect my kingdom, above all. "Listen, I've fallen out of favor with the sorceress, and she's cursed me."

"What did you do?" Oren asked, as though it was my fault.

I didn't blame the form of his question. Falling out of favor with the sorceress was often because one had displeased her or committed a crime, but that was not the case with me. "She's always disliked the magnitude of my power, but now, she's found a way to steal it with a demon."

Oren cursed. "What are you going to do?"

I pinched the bridge of my nose. "I've trapped the demon, but it's already begun to feed. I can't kill it without killing myself."

Oren groaned. "That's worse than I imagined."

Retracting my claws, I held up a finger. "There's an old legend about four relics, known as the tears of the gods. Their rare and potent magic could assist me in gaining freedom. I'm going to find them all, sever the bond, and trap the sorceress in her own domain. She's done enough damage."

"Some of it well deserved," Oren said, a dangerous note in his tone.

I paused; it was rare for anyone to take the sorceress' side unless they were under her spell. Still, Oren had a point. "True. In the beginning, she was instructed to keep the realms safe from corruption, and the punishments she dealt out were severe but deserved. However, as of late, she's enjoyed causing chaos for the sake of chaos. I believe she's finally sick on the magnitude of her power and has succumbed to corruption."

"I'm sure she would say the same about you," Oren said soberly. "I only say this because we are friends. I've been drunk on power, so blindsided by revenge that I became corrupt."

I shrugged, unbothered by the bite of those words. It was true. I was immortal, powerful, and ruthless, as a king should be. "From the tale you've told me, you were justified in your actions."

"In some, but not all of them," Oren admitted.

I raised my eyebrows. "It's not like you to admit you're wrong, but you got what you wanted in the end, didn't you?"

"I did, with the help of a mortal."

"That's what I'm after. This time, the sorceress has gone too far."

Oren crossed his arms. "Then you must stop her. Tell me about these ancient relics. Isn't there a cost to finding them?"

Discomfort shivered through me, a warning against seeking the relics, but I ignored it. My need was great, and this was the only way. "Aye, I've studied the legends and found the assumed location of each one. There is a condition, though."

"There's always an unsavory condition," Oren snorted.

I sighed. Nothing was easy, especially when it concerned magic. "True, otherwise the relics wouldn't be where they are today. The blood of a willing mortal is necessary to secure each one."

Oren chuckled. "In my experience, most mortals are very unwilling."

I plucked a string of my harp, listening to the vibrations echo into the silence. "A mortal of royal blood."

Oren scoffed. "Why *royal* blood? Is blood used to retrieve the relics?"

"A *female* of royal blood," I clarified. "She will be able to walk on sacred ground and retrieve the relics. Her purity will bless them and allow me to use them."

Oren was silent for a while. "I don't like this, Zekiel. From what you've told me, you are seeking an ancient bloodline. Rumor has it, the ancients were all killed out long ago. It will be difficult to find such a mortal. Is there no other way?"

I tampered down my anger, already well aware of

what Oren warned me against. I wasn't truly angry with him, only frustrated with the limitations on my freedom, how difficult my quest would be. Still, my words came out sharper than I intended. "Find me the Sorcerer of Music. That is the only other way."

Oren frowned. "You believe the power of song will be enough?"

"Not just any song: the *right* song. It will break the bond between the demon and myself and allow me to slay it. But no, I don't want to stop there. The sorceress must be punished, her throne taken down, and she, herself, locked away forever, bonded to a tower like the knights she's so fond of punishing."

Oren lifted his pipe again. "Then let me help you. Let me play."

I shook my head. "You've been through enough. Go, take your wife and travel to other realms. Return when it's safe."

Oren huffed. "So that's what you're going to do? Send everyone away and deal with this alone?"

"I am king. It's what I do."

"If you will not help me, I will give you one gift: the music to the old songs I know. Perhaps one of them will break the demon bond."

I bowed my head. "I will allow that one gift."

Oren stepped back, tone low. "If you fail, and that monster comes anywhere near me and my wife, I will unleash vengeance like the world has never seen."

In the past, I'd judged Oren's actions as dramatic,

particularly when I was calm, patient, and ready to strike when the opportune moment presented itself. My current situation left me impatient. I longed to use sweeping acts of magical power, for revenge was potent in my blood. "I'll vanquish this demon, and then I'll make the sorceress wish she'd never been born," I promised, squeezing my hand into a fist.

"Best of luck on your hunt," Oren said. "Although knowing you, your plan is already in motion."

I barred my fangs in a wolfish grin. "It is. Within a year, I'll be free."

Oren bowed his head and stepped back. "Be careful, Zekiel. Don't let the haze of revenge make you lose sight of what's important. I did once, and it nearly cost me everything."

2

CELESTE

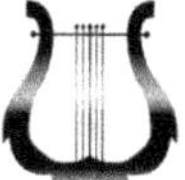

Frost crunched under my bare feet, and icicles stabbed into my exposed skin like tiny needles. My breath puffed out in a cloud as I ran, ducking under the shady boughs of sparse timbers, shaking a dusting of snow down like sugar onto my head. Behind me came the baying of hounds, their cries matching the frantic drumming of my heart.

Again, the words of the huntress came to me. *Run into the wood, Celeste. Get as far away as you can.*

A chill shot down my spine at the truth the huntress spoke when she entered my chamber in the middle of the night to execute my escape.

The king's death was no mistake. Word says it was poison, but we both know it was her.

The shock of those words took some time to reach my numb mind, because on some level, I'd known it was true, but I wanted to hide instead of deal with a battle I'd inevitably lose. Her next words, though, stunned me.

She wants to eat your heart because your beauty surpasses hers. If you want to live, run.

The huntress had taken my cloak and covered it in boar's blood as a decoy, but the hounds were smart and quickly caught my trail. When I heard their cries, I'd stripped out of my gown and ripped it to shreds, setting a false path for them to follow.

Now, I fled, searching for shelter in the wood before they found me.

The haunted forest to the north of the castle was fabled for its mysterious creatures with wicked intentions, but I had to take my chances. I prayed the soldiers hunting me would be too frightened to enter, that I could weave through the dangerous wood before any wicked creatures found me.

A branch loomed in front of me, and I tripped over it, scratching my arms and legs as I tumbled into a briar. The scent of molding old leaves invaded my senses, and even though it was warmer here, away from the keen breeze, sharp, brittle leaves poked at my skin.

I lay a moment, letting my heartrate settle to a dull thud as I listened. The baying of hounds grew distant, and sweet relief made my shoulders sag. They'd taken the bait and followed my torn clothing.

Untangling myself from the briar, I stood tall, turning to exit the woods. To my dismay, it was thicker than I expected, and each direction looked the same: menacing trees covered with ivy and a gloom that dripped down them like sap. Gray mist wafted from the forest floor like fingers of the undead, creeping over the fallen leaves and bracken.

My stomach twisted, but I spun again. Surely, I could find my way out. I would not let panic override my sensibilities. A tree branch broke somewhere nearby, and I whirled to face it, only to hear a low growl followed by a squeal. I pressed a hand to my chest, fingers trembling as the ancient wood sprang to life. It might have been my imagination, but shadows shifted toward me, shaped like humans with tails and horns.

An awareness came over me that if I didn't find shelter, I'd likely freeze to death in the wood, and my flight would have been for naught.

Swallowing down my indecision, I chose a direction and took a step, one after the other, but the more I walked, the denser the foliage became. The trees moved closer, the bushes grew thicker, and ivy crawled across the ground like snakes, wrapping around my ankles. Impossible stories whispered in the back of my mind.

Never enter the forest of the unholy, for a grim fate awaits and you will be stolen.

This was a mistake. My clever idea to outwit the queen's men only sealed my doom. Tears burned the back of my eyes as I walked, and my entire body shook, not just from the cold, but from fear. With each step, the wood grew darker, and at one point, I turned to go back, but the trees were against me, shutting the way out. A thick hedge formed behind me, sap dripping from the leaves like blood.

I shivered and forced myself to keep going, despite the thorns that tore at my flesh and the vines that curled up my legs. This was my fate. My father, the king, had been poisoned, and the plants in this haunted forest would devour me. My steps grew slower and heavier as the vines moved up my thighs, squeezing, the hem of my shift turning black with sap.

Wrapping my arms around my chest, I stopped, a final plea leaving my lips. "If you are real, spirits of the forest, please, help me. I want to live."

Suddenly, a silver light flashed and the ground beneath me shook. A cry split the air as the vines released me and the hedge backed away. My chest went tight as I glanced behind me, noticing I now stood at the edge of a tiny clearing.

The forest is full of tricks; be sure to keep your wits.

I took a step back, fingers reaching for the once-menacing hedges as they receded further. A scream rose in my throat as the ground opened, a horse and rider springing up as though fleeing from hell itself.

I caught a fleeting vision of a giant black battle horse, with red eyes and flaring nostrils. On its back rode a horned monster, one clawed hand reaching for me.

With a cry, I stumbled away, fleeing for my life as the horse and rider bore down on me. The trees continued to back away, leaving an open expanse for me to run, but no place to hide.

My sore feet throbbed, my breath rasping until I tasted iron in the back of my throat, and yet, I forced myself onward until I thought I would vomit from exertion.

The thunder of hooves pounded the ground, and flecks of mud flew up in front of me. Suddenly, a whip curled around my ankle, ripping me off my feet. All the breath left my body as I landed heavily on my side, fingers digging into the dirt for support as I gasped and choked.

The shadowed monster moved over me, and though my vision was hazy, I still made out his human-like face, deep gray eyes, and moonlight hair that flowed down to his waist. His chest was bare underneath his cloak, and my face flamed at the impropriety of it, though I had bigger concerns at the moment.

He was only half-monster, horns on his head and claws at the end of one hand. The other was covered in a black glove. He rolled me onto my back, studying me with an indescribable expression.

My chest heaved as I took in his beauty. He was a dark angel, sent from a realm of nightmares to torment me with attractive features and only a hint of the monster that twisted beneath the surface.

As those intense eyes studied me, a calm sense of resignation came over me. His gloved hand slid around my leg, removing the whip, and then, without a word, he swung me over his shoulder.

The world tilted upside down as he carried me to that terrible horse, and then my senses returned. I screamed as he mounted it, laying me across his lap like a sacrifice. His bare hand instantly wrapped around my throat, claws just shy of nicking my delicate skin. When he spoke, his voice was low and sensual. "Do not scream. The shadow walkers will hear."

"How are they worse than you?" I whispered.

A ghost of a smirk crossed his lips. Instead of replying, he leaned over and spoke a command.

We dove into the hole in the ground, and my world went black.

3

ZEKIEL

She wasn't supposed to be pretty. My spies had told me she was ugly, a scorned princess with no friends, locked in a room because she was in mourning and the queen hated her. In truth, she was beautiful, tall and willowy, long limbs and golden-brown skin, big brown eyes, and a wide, kissable mouth.

I shouldn't have used the whip on her, but hesitation would cost me, and time was of the essence. It was only a miracle we got away without the sorceress' spies finding us. They lurked in the wood, eager for blood, and the princess' clothes—if they could be called clothes—were covered in tree sap. If I hadn't stolen her, they would have ravaged her.

Yet, the look of defeat and resignation in those dark eyes haunted me, as well as the way she'd lain still as I turned her over, as though she had no fight left. That had come later, and now she slumped in my arms as I carried her through the dark halls, aware of the lurking evil presence in the bowels of the earth. My hand throbbed in pain, a reminder I needed to play, to find a song to drive the demon away.

"How did I do?" a sing-song tone rang out and a flash of pale pink light warned me I was no longer alone.

My jaw clenched, but I managed to nod to the fairy who flew over my head, wings beating as fast as a hummingbird's as she zipped down the hall, anxiously zipping back and forth. "Hada, you did well. I appreciate your assistance in procuring a princess from the mortal realm. Will you be leaving now?"

Hada had the gall to land on my shoulder, probably because my hands were full and I could not flick her into the wall. "This is the princess? She's filthy. Well, I'm interested now. Let me help a bit longer. You can't have this filth tramping around your castle. Besides, my fairies are handy with needle and thread."

"You try my patience, but you have a point," I relented. "See that she is clean and dressed, then find me when you're done."

"As you wish," Hada cackled.

I blew her off my shoulder, smirking as she fell, catching herself at the last moment. Fairies were fickle and fond of eavesdropping, often turning up when least expected and especially where they weren't wanted. Hada had overheard one too many private conversations and knew too much about my plans. I wished she'd leave of her own accord and take the irritation of her presence with her, but she just wouldn't go.

"Don't you want to know how I found her?" Hada asked, wisely staying behind me.

"No, I don't. It's none of my business, and you have many other fairies to brag to."

"Fine, I'll keep my secrets to myself," Hada huffed. "But if you knew. . .if only you knew. . ."

I pressed my lips together, ignoring her weaseling. If only Hada knew how desperate I was to get rid of her and her people without suffering the ill consequences. Knowledge was power, and Hada had far too much. A cold dread went through me. What if there was another, darker reason she stayed?

4

CELESTE

I dreamed I was sailing, except I wasn't in a boat but in the water, floating on my back in a sea of white lotus flowers. A musky perfume filled the air, and I blinked, almost swallowing a mouthful of water. I spat and jerked up, my eyes flying open as I realized this was no dream.

Indeed, I lay in a shallow stone pool inside some kind of cavern, and I was naked.

Panic filled me as I crossed my hands over the swells of my breasts, searching for the horned monster who'd stolen me, but I was alone in the cavern. Stone walls sloped into the darkness, but they shimmered with silver light, as though gems were trapped in layers of rock, burning to shine their radiance on me.

On a bench was a white towel but no clothes, nor any signs of my dirty shift. It's not that I wanted to put that filthy rag on again, but I wanted *something* to wear.

Keeping my eyes on the cavern entrance, I climbed out of the pool and dried off. I was clean, as though someone had scrubbed my skin, and while my legs were clearly scratched, someone had taken the time to cleanse them.

Was it him?

A bolt of hot fury shot through me at the idea of him taking advantage of my body while I was unconscious. I needed to confront him and demand answers, but I was out of my element. What would he do with me and why had he stolen me, aside from carnal pleasure?

My face heated, and I forced the idea of being taken by a monster out of my mind.

Lifting my chin, I crept toward the opening of the cavern, wincing as my sore feet padded across the slick stones. A rock mirrored my reflection, and I paused, my fingers going to the shorn ends of my short hair. Cuts from the malicious forest crisscrossed my golden-brown skin, my dark brown eyes wide and hollow, and my once curvy body now too thin. Self-consciously, I tucked the short ends of my hair behind my ears, swallowing down my tears.

Ever since my father's death, the queen—my stepmother, Vivian—had locked me in my room, claiming I was a threat to the kingdom. At times, she forgot to feed me and only occasionally had she visited. At first, she seemed afraid of me, but each time, she grew bolder, her threats turning from meaningless words to physical abuse. She'd half-starved me, cut off my hair, and even had the guards hold me down while she used her knife on me.

As the huntress had told me, the queen was obsessed with beauty and ruling. None could be better than her, and, as the heir to the crown, I was her rival. Now I saw those visits for what they were: she was gaining the courage to cut out my heart in an arcane ritual only used by witches and those in league with darker forces. I shuddered, wondering if the half-monster who'd stolen me was in league with something dark and deadly.

The melody of a stringed instrument broke through my gloomy thoughts. If there was music, there must be someone civil in this place. Leaving the mirror, I followed the passageway out, noting the glimmer of gold beneath my bare toes.

A bend in the cavern gave way to a staircase, and I followed it up into a hall lit by torches. The stone floor turned to a velvet carpet beneath my feet. It was warm, a relief from my flight through frost. I'd hoped the warmth of spring would ease my escape, but the bite of winter still held.

As I walked, I considered where I might be and what had happened to the half-monster who dragged me through the ground. Perhaps it was only a fabrication, and the hole was a secret entrance to a tunnel connected to this fortress.

The lulling tones of the music grew louder; a harp, I

thought, as I stepped into a brightly lit room. I was alone, but a fire burned in the stone hearth, and the scent of food made my mouth water. A table—with enough chairs for six—sat near the entrance, a scroll and a pot of ink at one end. Gilded doors to a balcony were ajar, and from them came the sweet melody, making my heart ache with longing.

Enchanted, I wavered in the entrance until the music stopped and the horned monster who'd stolen me stepped into the room.

Those deep eyes arrested mine and, drawing a sharp breath, I took a step back. The angles of his face were sharp, as though carved from crystal. His skin was bronze, and his open robe displayed the tight muscles of his chest and abs. In one hand, he carried a golden harp that he sat on a side table, fingers flexing as he gazed at me. "Where are your clothes?"

My mouth fell open at the absurdity of his question, and indignation replaced my timidness. "I came to ask you the same thing." I pointed an accusing finger at him. "You're the one who left me naked in a pool without a shred of clothing in sight."

He rubbed the back of his neck as though ashamed and glanced at the fire. "That was the fairies. I instructed them to wake you and make clothing suitable for your time here. You must have left before they finished."

I raised my eyebrows. What kind of lie was that? "You want me to believe there are such beings as fairies, and that they are responsible for my lack of clothing? Just admit it; you took advantage of me when I was unconscious."

He stiffened and his face darkened. "Dare you accuse me of such evil?" he growled.

I took a step back, suddenly remembering my place.

The half-monster moved to the balcony and called, "Hada."

A moment later, a ball of rosy light winked inside, and I reached for the wall to steady myself. As he'd said, there was, indeed, a fairy. She was just the size of my hand, with delicate wings, clothes made of leaves, and a saucy smile she threw at my host. "She ran off. . ." the fairy started, then caught sight of me. "Oh, there you are. We came back with your garment, and you were gone."

I bit my lower lip, words failing me. I'd been wrong. Fairies existed.

"Bring it here," my host instructed.

"As you wish." The fairy stuck out her tongue in a shocking act of direct insubordination and flew back outside.

"Sit." My host gestured to the table.

Still tongue-tied and shocked by the fairy's behavior, I took a seat, my back to the door.

He sat down on the other end, picked up the quill, and began to write. "This will be the contract between you and me."

"Contract?" I mustered, my mouth dry.

"Yes. You fled for your life into my arms."

My face warmed. That was debatable; he'd stolen me.

"You seek safety from your pursuers, and I can offer that in exchange for a year of service."

My eyebrows shot up, and I said the first words that came to mind. "I won't be your whore."

He paused, hand in the air, a faint hint of amusement spreading across his face as he stared at me. "Do I look in need of a whore?"

"Err..." I fumbled. "I wanted to be quite clear."

"Then I will be quite clear as well. I need you to retrieve four items for me. After doing so, you will be free to return to where you came from, or elsewhere, if you desire."

"I..."

"Failure to sign the contract means I will return you to the forest and let the trees and shadow walkers have their way with you."

The last words were menacing. He left me with no choice. I clutched the towel, aware I had nothing to bargain with.

My host went on. "You will have food, shelter, and clothing for the duration of our time together, as well as additional payment after successful completion of each task."

I licked my dry lips. "I accept."

He put down the quill and picked up a letter opener. "Come. Sign."

Standing on leaden legs, I forced myself to cross to him, desperately trying to hold up the towel as I went. The wicked end of the letter opener winked in the light as he held it toward me.

"Prick your finger and sign with blood."

Now that I was up close, I couldn't drag my gaze away from his black horns or the shine of his moonlight hair. His manly scent made something shift inside me, and heat flamed my cheeks as I tucked the ends of the towel under my armpits to prick my finger.

Drops of dark blood spilled out, marring the parchment. I hastily signed and stepped back, desperate to put more proximity between him and me.

My host sprinkled dust on the parchment to set it then glanced at me. "What is it? You have a question?"

"Since we will be working together, what should I call you?"

He smirked. "You may call me Zekiel."

5

ZEKIEL

The princess stared at me, her lips moving as though silently repeating my name. An awareness hovered between us and I instinctively leaned forward, as though to catch the sweet notes of her voice.

Now that I'd gotten more than two words out of her, I liked the haunting tones of her melodic voice, as though she were about to break into song. It stirred something within me, luring me in, and I wanted to hear those throaty tones again.

Instead, she stepped back, one hand self-consciously resting on the towel, reminding me of her near-nakedness. Dropping my gaze, I let it sweep over her exposed skin.

When she'd first entered the room, her make-shift gown had taken me off guard, and I tried not to stare, but gods, I was but a man with desires untapped, and her comment about not being my whore—as if I'd choose a runaway in a dark wood—had only brought the idea to the forefront. Annoying, how the very thought of making her my lover hadn't entered my mind until she mentioned it, and now it was all I could think about.

The firelight caught the hues of her rich brown skin, and my gaze lingered on her long arms and legs. Her chin quivered, and I forced my gaze up to meet the depths of her dark brown eyes. A hollowness hovered there, a hint of fear and a spark of defiance. Her delicate features were beautiful yet fragile, reminding me of a hunted animal, exhausted yet still fighting, despite knowing death was imminent.

A drop of water slipped off her drying curls and landed on her bare shoulder. I watched it roll toward the column of her neck, and the idea of licking it off made my cock twitch. Damn the fairies and their lack of respect, leaving her unclothed like this in my presence. It was likely they'd done the act out of spite. I needed to stop giving them a chance to show their loyalty. They were mischievous at the best of times, but even worse now that their allegiance didn't lie with me.

Waving my hand, claws on display, I gestured to the table. "Have a seat. Hinko prepared a meal. After you eat, I'll show you to your room."

"My room?"

My lip curled at her surprise. "I would not have you

sleep on the floor." I returned my gaze to the contract, because there was something beguiling about her that left me wanting. The faint scent of blood rose, reminding me I had work to do. "Besides, according to the terms of the contract, I owe you food, shelter, and clothing."

She nodded, and a moment later, Hinko swept into the room.

Her eyes went wide as he slid a tray in front of her, gave me a short bow, and disappeared as quickly as he'd come. I supposed gnomes who served meals weren't a common occurrence in the kingdom she'd fled from, but she seemed to regain herself quickly and began to eat.

I watched her out of the corner of my eye, pretending to write while my mind was a flurry of thoughts, emotion ripping through me as the weight of what would happen next sank in. I gently clinked my claws together. She had arrived, and now, my quest for revenge would begin.

6

CELESTE

The sound of the latch turning startled me awake. I dragged my eyes open from the deep sleep I'd been in, my breath suddenly turning shallow at the idea of someone entering the chamber I slept in.

As promised, after a warm meal, Zekiel had led me to my room. The concave chamber was dark, aside from a tiny fire that burned in the hearth, the floor covered with thick rugs, and a bed a few feet from the fireplace. Heavy drapery covered the window, and when I'd moved it, I'd seen nothing but the black of night.

He'd bade me rest after my ordeal and left, but shortly afterward, the fairies flew in, bringing a thin, gossamer gown with them. They buzzed around me, braiding my hair and scolding me for leaving the bath before they could return. They brought salve for my bruises, and I'd thanked them politely, then asked if they had anything else for me to wear, aside from the see-through gown. With that, they'd told me it was a nightdress and left, as though insulted.

Now, my fingers crept around the fur blanket, wondering if the person who entered wished me ill. It was dark, but I glimpsed a shadow moving along the wall and heard a curse as it stumbled over something. I stiffened. The voice was male, and my heart raced. Surely Zekiel knew I was in here. Why would he enter the room in the dead of night?

My chest went tight, and fears wormed their way through my mind. Perhaps he'd been lying to me, and I was to be his whore after all. If so, I shouldn't lie here and take it. I needed to get up and defend myself, but fear paralyzed my body.

The sound of flint striking stone came and then light flared up, displaying the face of a man. He appeared human, with short black hair and sea-blue eyes that widened when he saw me. His mouth dropped open, and he stumbled back.

"Apologies, I have the wrong room," he slurred his words as though drunk, then turned—with another muttered curse—as he banged into something else. He finally made his way back to the door. "Forgive me. Please forget this happened."

The door clicked shut as he left, taking the light with him, and I was in darkness again, my heart pounding.

In a moment, I was out of bed, fumbling across the room.

I slid the bolt into place. Feeling somewhat safer, I returned to the warmth of the covers, but it was a long while before I fell back asleep, my mind racing with the mysteries that lay within the strange realm I'd fallen into.

When I did wake, light shone on my face, and the familiar crackle of the fire soothed my nerves until I recalled I wasn't in the palace anymore but in some strange fortress. I bolted upright, taking in the open curtains, the fire burning, a pair of leathers laid out at the foot of the bed, and an overturned table with a white scroll lying by the door.

A sense of unease overcame me as the hairs on my neck prickled. Even though I'd bolted the door, someone had entered, opened the curtains, brought me clothes, and even left a tray of what I assumed was breakfast. I frowned, wondering if it was the fairies again. I was starting to dislike the way they constantly invaded my privacy, especially when I was unconscious.

Still, the clothes looked promising, so I dressed first, pulling on a skirt that fell almost to my ankles, a white shirt, and over it, a leather jerkin. The clothes were warm and, unlike what I wore in the palace, easy to put on without the help of my maid. Making my way to the looking glass, I ran my fingers through my hair but there was no need: the braids the fairies had woven held and the rest of my hair poofed whichever way it wanted. Scowling, I gave up and turned my attention to the scroll.

The dark stain of a red seal covered one side, and I gingerly lifted it up, making out the shape of a harp with snakes crossed underneath, somewhat menacing. My fingers hovered on the seal, wondering if I should break it. The scroll might not be for me. Perhaps it belonged to the man who'd entered my room last night and he'd dropped it in his haste to leave. Maybe it was a clue, a key to my location.

Curiosity won over my sense of propriety. Sliding my finger under the seal, I unfurled the scroll and read.

Celeste Elvera, Princess of Domingo, enters into a blood-binding contract with Zekiel Jude, the King of Hearts.

Princess Celeste agrees to complete four tasks for the King of Hearts over a period of one year in exchange for food, shelter and clothing.

The specifics of each task are to be determined at the discretion of the King of Hearts, with additional payment rendered upon successful completion of each.

If either party defaults on the contract, the penalty is blood and a reversion to the circumstance they were in before signing the agreement.

. . .

My chest squeezed as a haze of fear and confusion enveloped me. The scroll was for me, and Zekiel, that half-monster, not only knew my birth name, but he was a *king*!

I staggered to a seat, my mind racing as I raked my memory for rumors and old tales I'd read about the haunted forest and the monsters that lived underneath it, banished from the face of the land because of their evil ways. Had I entered some shadow mockery of the land above, where horned creatures ruled? How had the king discovered my name so quickly, unless he was working for the queen? What if he meant to return me to her after I finished the four tasks for him?

Crossing my arms, I rocked back and pinched my thigh, hard. Instead of feeling sorry for myself, I needed to come up with a plan and act, before I fell prey to yet another nefarious plan from a wicked royal. Standing, I shook out my skirts and tucked the scroll into them. I'd confront him, see what he had to say for himself, and then plan my escape.

Jerking open the door—which wasn't bolted anymore, much to my chagrin—I strode out and promptly bowled over a pink-haired creature.

The creature let out a shirk of dismay as I recovered my balance, taking in bright blue eyes in a round face framed by pink pigtails. It was a female, about three feet tall, also wearing leather, with a few tools tucked into her belt.

"Who are you?" I exclaimed, my mind racing. A word hovered on my tongue as I took her in. Was she a dwarf? A gnome?

"I'm Petra," she grinned, showing off a row of perfectly straight white teeth. "What a meeting. I meant to knock on your door to see if you'd finished your meal yet, and look at you, all dressed and ready to go."

"Er. . .I'm sorry about that. I was in a hurry and didn't look," I apologized.

Father said never to apologize to the help, because it made one appear weak. In my opinion, they were people too, and I'd decided kindness went a long way. Besides, even though they were paid to help me, they could also tie a corset too tightly, spit in my food, fain innocence when the fire wasn't lit, and employ all kinds of other passive-aggressive strategies. It didn't help that I wasn't popular in the palace, so my maids weren't happy to assist me, and the lords and ladies ignored me as though I were some cursed oddity, which meant I had to make friends where I could. In this strange new place, I needed to ensure I had help if I were to escape.

"In a hurry to go where?" Petra giggled, hand on the door.

"To find the king. . .Zekiel," I said, although it seemed wrong to use his name without a formal title in front of it.

Something shifted on Petra's friendly face, a slight

darkening I thought, but it was gone in a flash. Had I said something wrong? "You're the princess, aren't you?"

"It's just Celeste," I blurted out, biting my tongue instantly. I wasn't supposed to be giving out my true name, but I hated that she, too, knew I was a princess. "Perhaps you can help me. He didn't tell me much about this place. Where am I?"

"You'll have to speak with him directly." Petra bit her bottom lip, as though she wanted to say more. "Good luck."

She disappeared into the room, leaving the door ajar. My stomach growled at the idea of breakfast, but I could eat later. It was more important to gain clarity on what might be going on.

As I continued down the hall, concave walls sloped around me and silver shimmered, a dazzling hint of what lay beneath the stone. Could I be in some kind of cavern that opened into a mine? It was clear there was wealth here.

Murmured voices broke my thoughts, and I quickened my pace, wondering what I should say to the king to make him understand my position. The voices grew louder, coming from an open door. I thought it might be the same room where I'd signed the contract, but I couldn't be sure. I slowed down as an argument floated to my ears.

"This is reckless. Sure to get us all killed," a tenor male voice spoke adamantly.

A female laugh cut through his biting remark, although I sensed some bitterness in it. “We’re all going to die one way or another, so why not in this reckless endeavor? I, for one, stand by your decision, Zekiel.”

“We would not be this reckless, as you call it, Ryder, without great need. Do you stand by my side?”

“You have my allegiance. I was merely stating a fact. . .”

“You were making sure we were aware of the dangers, but is that not why you are in my employment? Because danger calls to you and you cannot stay away?”

A snorted laugh came again, the female clearly unbothered by the tension between the two males, one I guessed to be Zekiel, the other, Ryder.

“It’s more than danger calling our names this time. It’s pure evil, and Yosa, you of all people shouldn’t laugh. One day, our deeds will catch up with us. Perhaps this is why we are cursed with such blighted evil.”

“Not true,” the female, Yosa, protested. “All of this is because the sorceress is jealous. Revenge is the only way forward. Where is Oren, Zekiel? Isn’t he going to use his magical flute?’

“That damned pipe,” Zekiel cursed. “It would bring the legions of hell to our doorstep. He is gone. I sent him away because this is an evil he shouldn’t have to deal with, especially after—”

"Right," Yosa interrupted. "Shall we go? Or do we get to meet her first?"

"It's better that you didn't," Zekiel said.

I shrank against the wall as the door opened wider, but before I could run, out sauntered the man who'd entered my chamber last night. He was tall and lean, with thick black hair, a hooked nose, deep-set eyes, and a day's worth of stubble covering his chin. He wore leather and carried a bow, a quiver of arrows on his back, knives in his belt. What drew my attention, though, was the gray hawk that sat on his shoulder, staring at me with beady, golden eyes.

I froze against the wall like an intruder, but the man only gave me a brief nod as he passed, as though we were ghosts in the night, merely going about our business.

The next person to leave the room was the woman, Yosa. She was actually still speaking to Zekiel, but I didn't catch exactly what she said as she tumbled out, all curls and curves.

Bright green eyes winked at me, and she smiled, her entire face lighting up when she saw me. "Oh! You must be the retriever. I'm Yosa; it's a pleasure to meet you. Finally, another female in this male-filled castle. I'm not complaining," she grinned, "but it will be nice to have another woman around for a bit."

"I...hello," I managed under the onslaught of her words.

"I'm sorry," Yosa pressed a hand to her mouth, eyes

sparkling. "I talk far too much. It's both a blessing and a curse. I'm sure we'll have time for a proper chat later."

She dashed off before I could stop her, calling after Ryder to wait for her. He didn't so much as turn around, and I could have sworn he quickened his pace.

When I turned back around, Zekiel was glaring at me.

7

CELESTE

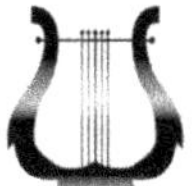

He leaned against the doorframe, arms crossed, purple shirt open, displaying an expanse of muscular chest. Moonlight-colored hair hung almost to his waist and glowed against the shimmer of light on the walls. Those gray eyes studied me as though I were a morsel he was considering whether to devour or toss away.

Words failed me, so I reached into my pocket and held up the scroll. Swallowing hard, I was the first to break the silence. "How do you know who I am?"

His eyes narrowed. "I wouldn't have stolen you if I didn't know who you were."

It was my turn to cross my arms, anger making me bold. "But how? Why didn't you say anything yesterday? You led me to believe I was safe here, but for all I know, you could be working with the queen."

"You signed with blood, and blood does not lie.

Besides, I gave you a choice to return to the forest or work for me. You choose the latter of your own free will. If you had chosen the former, I would have returned you to the world above."

I huffed, still determined to be angry despite the truth of his words. "What kind of king takes pleasure in stealing a princess from the land above and dragging her down here to be tormented by fairies? Where am I anyway, and what kind of terrible tasks do you have in mind?"

His face changed and he stepped closer, eyes sparking, not with anger but with something else I couldn't name. "I don't take pleasure in stealing. I do what I must, but you are correct. I am the king of this land, and you have given yourself to me."

My mouth dropped open and the scroll slipped from my fingers. When he said it like that, it sounded almost nefarious. "I had no choice," I sputtered.

Bending down, he plucked the scroll from the floor and pressed it back into my hands. The warmth of his fingers drew my gaze, along with the acknowledgment that he had retracted his claws. He remained there, fingers around my wrist, so close that all I needed to do was lean forward to press my lips against his collarbone.

A pulse of heat passed through my lower belly, and I yanked my gaze away from his bare chest. Why was I tempted by the idea of kissing him? He was a monster who'd tricked me; I should hate him.

"You always have a choice," he said. "That is why I asked you to sign the contract rather than force you. Now, it is time to go."

"Go where?" I breathed.

"Your first task," he clarified. Letting go of me, he stepped back.

My mouth went dry. "Already?"

He raised an eyebrow. "It is why you're here, is it not?"

"Yes, I just thought. . ." I trailed off, not sure what, exactly, I thought. "Are the two others coming with us?"

A slight frown played about his mouth. "So, you were eavesdropping?"

My face flamed with heat. "I had no intention. I heard voices and they walked out just as..."

He raised his gloved hand, waving me off. I glanced between his bare hand and the gloved one. What is he hiding? Some sort of deformity?

Again came the reminder I was in some strange place and had to be careful.

"You will meet them again soon enough. I do not pretend to work alone."

"You are a king, aren't you?" The word slipped from my lips, acknowledging his status.

Again, those gray eyes studied me, hidden emotion shifting through them. "You will call me Zekiel and nothing else."

It was my turn to frown. My father would have

someone whipped if they dared to address him with such familiarity. "Are you ashamed of who you are? Your status?"

He stepped back, a hint of amusement playing across his face. "You are quite inquisitive for one so angry with me for knowing who you are. Come, I will take you back to the room that was prepared for you."

"What about the task?"

"I have a few items to finish up before we leave. Eat, relax, or whatever it is princesses do. There will be plenty of time for conversation."

Conversation was the one thing I wasn't very good at. Father had called me an odd princess, and he often hid me away from court so as not to embarrass him. Bitter thoughts plagued my memory, how he'd chosen his beautiful queen with perfect court decorum, someone who wouldn't embarrass him with thoughtless outbursts.

The pain of what I'd lost overwhelmed me as I blindly followed Zekiel down the shimmering hall.

He left me in the chamber without another word, and I lifted a hand to the bolt, then decided not to bother. It was clear whatever creatures wanted to enter the room would, without my say so. The overturned table had been rightened, the bed made, and the fire built up.

Petra? I suddenly felt guilty for running over my personal maid.

Dragging a chair to the window, which was high

up on the wall, I rose to my tiptoes to peer out the glass panes. As I expected, I was in some sort of cavern, for the window displayed the ground. Thick bushes grew on either side, framing the window and showing me little more than black dirt and grass. I was aware of an expanse beyond it, perhaps a meadow, for the light coming through was bright and vivid.

I blinked against it, wondering if I'd be able to return to the room where I'd signed the contract. There was a door to a patio, and perhaps an escape from all this. I'd almost been there when I'd run into Zekiel and his comrades. They appeared keen on helping him, and my stomach soured. They hadn't acted like he'd stolen them, and they'd voluntarily decided to work for him. Unlike him, they appeared human, no horns or claws or wings.

"There you are," a voice said.

I spun around, pressing a hand to my mouth to keep the scream of surprise inside. My eyes narrowed instantly as I took in the rosy glow of one of the fairies.

"I'm Hada," she said, landing on the bed and sending a sprinkle of fairy dust across it. "Don't stare at me like that. We've met a few times now, and each time, you give me that look."

I rearranged my face. "It's just...you keep appearing without announcing yourself and it's disconcerting, you flying through walls and all."

Hada snorted. "Why should I announce myself? I'm a fairy. I go where I please."

I already regretted the conversation. "I only meant…never mind. What can you tell me about this place?"

Hada spun in a circle. "How boring. I thought you might ask me something interesting."

"Interesting like what?"

"You know, something about the king. Never mind; I have a bit of advice for you." Hada fluttered her wings.

I clasped my hands together, stopping just short of rolling my eyes. I did not intend to take advice from a fairy who had no respect for boundaries or modesty, or that she was leaving a pile of dust on the bed. Yet, I had the sense she would not take no for an answer.

"What is your advice?"

Hada grinned. "What are you going to give me in exchange?"

"How do I know your advice is of value?"

"You're the one who is new to this realm."

Point taken. "What do you want?"

"The king has hired you to be a retriever; let's be honest, you're a thief for him."

I swallowed hard, hating my stupidity. The four tasks laid out in the contract were to steal for him. A sudden anger hardened my heart as the fairy continued.

"I can go anywhere in this place, except for the treasury. He has it under some kind of spell I cannot penetrate, but you'll be close to him and his work. He'll learn to trust you and you'll be able to weave through his spells. Retrieve a ruby for me, in the shape of an unbudded flower."

"Why? You work for him; why don't you just ask?"

"He took it from me to seal my allegiance to him. I take it back and I'll be free."

Free. "He stole you too?"

Hada snorted. "Zekiel isn't the kind of king who simply takes one at their word. He always takes something else to seal the bargain, and I want it back."

My mind stirred at the thought. "If that's the case, I don't want advice in exchange for stealing this jewel for you. I want you to help me escape."

A shriek of laughter escaped from Hada, and she threw herself on the bed, legs kicking in the air as she giggled. "Aren't you a funny one. Escape? There is no escape. You made a contract with him, so either you fulfill the terms or you die."

"Surely there's another way?"

Hada sobered up. "You're serious. Why yes, there might be a third option. Do we have a deal?"

I nodded once, unsure if this was a particularly wise choice. "Yes, I'll find the jewel, and you'll help me escape."

8

ZEKIEL

Candlelight flickered as I entered my sanctum, a circle of winking lights welcomed me into their midst. Seven columns stood in a circle, each one at my waist height, holding up a basin of water. They were mirrors, a way to watch the seven portals that guarded my realm, a way to gauge how much my magic had weakened, and what foul beasts might slip through the gates to terrorize my land.

Ryder was my hunter, and, with his men, guarded the portals against unsavory beasts. Still, some spies easily slipped through, and it was difficult to distinguish between friend or foe. Some monsters took on the form of non-humans, immortals like me, while others appeared as humans or faeries.

I'd long suspected that Hada and her fairies were working for someone else, but I couldn't figure out her end game. She helped me and irritated me all in the same breath, and not simply because of what I'd taken from her. No, the ruby stone didn't mean that much to them. True, it held a token of magic that was dangerous in the wrong hands, but I'd only taken it to seal their allegiance to me, and now I was loathe to return it.

Going to the basin in the center, I leaned over it, speaking the enchantment until the mist cleared and displayed the southern border of my kingdom, the portal I'd used to steal the princess from the haunted forest. Something was wrong. The portal was covered in a layer of ice, frozen, imprisoning me within this realm, keeping anyone and everyone else out, but trapping me all the same.

A whisper of disquiet moved through me, and I shifted to the next portal, my heart pounding as I whispered the enchantment, magic swirling, tightening around me like grasping fingers. It too was frozen over, closed, gone, as though a hidden menace had swept into my kingdom.

Fingers clenched, I moved to the next one, fury making me want to punch the column. It would do no good; I had to be quicker, smarter. My mind raced as I moved to the next portal and the next, each one cracked and closed. Did the sorceress' power extend that far, or was someone else in my realm? I should have felt it the moment they entered, but my judgment was clouded, the potency of my magic waning, sucked away as though I were being bled dry.

I still had time, didn't I? There was only one way I

could leave, a way that would be taxing. I frowned, raking my mind for answers. The portals didn't matter to Ryder, or Yosa for that matter. He'd see that she was safely there and back. While he was gone, the hunters would need to rally against whatever force threatened my borders, without magic.

Celeste.

I was certain she was the answer, and I was grateful I'd found her yesterday. If I hadn't before the border closed…no, this had been done purposefully.

Stripping off my clothes, I strode from the hall of portals to my chamber, trying to rid myself of my agitation. It was no use dwelling on what was out of my control, especially since I had a plan, a way to fix everything. I just needed to focus, stay calm, and stick with it. Discovering the closed portals had been a blow, and I wished for a distraction to take my mind off it.

Celeste.

Something had happened between us in the hall, a slight shift that sent a bolt of lust zinging through me. What was it about her that broke down my barriers and made me feel desire again? No, this was not the time for emotional upheaval. I was hard, relentless, cold when I needed to be, focused solely on what benefited my kingdom.

Still, it was a relief to take my mind off my problems, to focus on something else.

Naked, I leaned over the fireplace, resting my forearm on the mantle, taking my cock in my fist.

She'd been quite clear that she wasn't looking for a lover, so I needed to keep my hands off her. This release would give me self-control for the long journey ahead.

Closing my eyes, I let my mind drift, thinking of soft curves and the warmth of flesh on flesh, the fiction of movement, throaty moans. Pure unbridled lust overcame me, but it was better I did this behind closed doors than acting on impulse when I was with her.

It took but a moment, and then I was panting, a sheen of sweat covering my body. Moving to the wash basin, I quickly cleaned myself and dressed.

Except I didn't feel sated. If anything, I wanted something real.

9

CELESTE

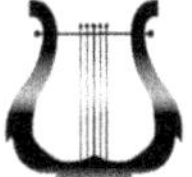

I'd barely finished breakfast when Zekiel came for me. He announced himself with a light tap on the door, and I opened it only to drown in the depths of his gaze.

He'd dressed since I'd last seen him: a crisp black shirt that hid his chest, dark boots, and a black cloak. One hand carried a bag of sorts, and he tilted his head, studying me as though he had an inkling of the deal I'd made with Hada.

Briefly, I wondered what kind of action he'd take when he discovered my treachery. He was no king of mine, only a half-monster who'd stolen me. I quickly forced thoughts of the blood-signed contract out of my mind.

"Are you ready?" he asked, his voice a low bass.

I sighed. "As I'll ever be."

He handed me a cloak. "Put this on and follow me."

The cloak was warm, and I fumbled to fasten it around my shoulders as I followed him down the passageway. Darkness converged into thick shadows, and I had a distinct feeling that despite the silver lights in the stone, something malicious was watching us.

Stone stairs led down, deep into the rock, and my throat closed, as though the weight of the earth pressed upon my shoulders. Occasionally, brightly colored tapestries appeared on the walls, lit up by flickering torchlight. The woven scenes depicted monsters and naked, winged creatures, both male and female, conjoining in endless pursuits of pleasure. Dancing. Drinking. Feasting. Making love.

I wondered who had taken the time to weave all those scenes and why they hung in passageways instead of a great hall, where many would see them.

The further down we went, the colder it became, until I was grateful for the leathers clinging to my body and the warmth of the cloak. The ominous sense of oppression tightened around us until we came to a stop before a wall of sheer rock. I craned my head back, aware of pale lights glowing above us, as though we stood in an entryway.

I glanced at Zekiel, who had been silent thus far. Questions pressed against my mind, but I held back, waiting, watching.

He placed his bare hand against the stone and spoke a few words in a haunting, musical tongue. Magical words, I assumed, for the rock shuddered and swung open, revealing a tunnel.

I had the sense that perhaps I should be impressed, but a shiver ran through me.

More pale lights hovered around us, and I became aware of a melody of hammers repeatedly striking stone, making my ears ring in a manner that was almost painful.

Fingertips grazed the small of my back as Zekiel guided me through the tunnel, his voice rumbling as he spoke. "Welcome to Irradiance, the kingdom of midnight."

"This is your kingdom?" I confirmed, watching the light at the end of the tunnel. It wasn't daylight but something else, bright and homey.

"Aye," he confirmed, removing his hand but remaining by my side.

I missed his touch—which shouldn't have been possible—but it was comforting. I tucked that thought away, because I shouldn't dwell on such things.

Moments later, we walked from the archway of the tunnel into an enormous cavern.

Obsidian walls towered above us, shooting higher than the eye could see. There were ladders and stone staircases, tunnels disappearing further into the rock, and a colony of gnomes working in some kind of unspoken rhythm. A low hum of activity came from voices, hammers, and song.

Crystals glittered in the stone, outshining the torchlight, which was the pale glow I'd seen. Diamonds, crimson rubies, midnight-colored sapphires, emeralds, amethysts, citrine, and other gems I could not name twinkled like a cluster of endless stars, filling the cavern with beauty.

This wasn't just a kingdom. It was an entire *world*.

It took me a moment to realize Zekiel was speaking, pride in his tone. "This is the underworld, or at least a portion of it. Irradiance lies beneath the crust of the land, where the roots of the trees dive deep and the soul of each body of water begins. This is the place where precious stones are mined, and creatures with weak eyes hide from the brilliance of sunshine."

Indeed, florescent mushrooms sprung from the dirt, and white and yellow creatures flitted back and forth. I thought some of them were moths, while others looked like fairies, like Hada.

Pressing a hand to my heart, I stared, my entire body throbbing with awareness and a desire for these treasures.

My father's kingdom also had mines, but they were dirty places to work, with low light and bad air. Many citizens got sick or even died from working underground for so long, and the taskmasters drove them hard.

Mines were for the poor or prisoners, but this was no such place. It was a kingdom, not of dust and dirt, but of beauty, and a buzz of excitement thrummed in the air.

The knowledge of just how wealthy and powerful Zekiel was made me feel weak. Awe tinged my voice when I managed to speak. "This is all yours?"

"This is not what you expected, is it?" He leaned closer to me, his breath like chocolate as he whispered in my ear.

I shivered, suddenly uncomfortable at our proximity, not because I wanted him to move away. No, I was afraid of what being near to him might lead to, what it made me want. A fluttering of desire brushed through my belly like the delicate wings of a butterfly. I bit my tongue, determined to taper down that sensation, unsure why Zekiel's presence brought it out of me. "The gnomes work for you?"

"This is home to the gnomes too, for their kingdom was taken over by a monster."

His words were matter-of-fact, and I studied his angular face, thinking on what Hada had told me. "You mean they made a deal with you to work here, and, in exchange, you asked them to do something for you?"

Gray eyes glittered in the low light. "You catch on quickly. Yes, it is a mutually beneficial deal. They are content, and so am I."

I didn't quite believe him, because if he was content, why was I here? An inkling told me something was wrong in a kingdom that, by all appearances, was perfect. I craned my neck to see further, but when I took a step forward, my boots scrapped against the rock and a shimmer rose. I leaped back, staring.

Zekiel chuckled. “It’s gem dust.” He squatted to pick up the fine grains and run them through his fingers. “It gets everywhere. If we stay too long in one place, you’ll be glittering like one of the jewels.”

I smiled at that vision, then tried not to, recalling I was supposed to be furious with him for stealing me and tricking me into that contract. Still, it was the most relaxed and at ease, he’d been with me—was this his normal behavior? “All this time, we’ve been underground?” I asked.

“No, but it is difficult to explain to mortals. You are no longer in the realm you used to be in. I brought you through a portal to my kingdom.”

My mind flashed back to the red-eyed horse leaping out of the ground. So *that* was a portal?

“How do I get back?” I asked bluntly.

Zekiel raised an eyebrow, then turned away from me, moving down a path. “You don’t.”

I’d said the wrong thing and his sudden talkativeness faded. Frowning, I followed him down the passageway, wondering what he wanted me to steal when he had all this. He could easily pay for anything he desired, so why did he need me?

The gnomes waved when they saw us, those nearby ceasing work to smile and bow. Their clothes and faces shone with dust, but I noticed the glow wasn’t merely skin deep. It was the luster of dreams and wealth, as if they were bewitched by the gems.

I did not blame them at all.

Zekiel slowed to walk beside me, sometimes lifting his hand to the small of my back to steer me in the right direction. A tingling went down my spine each time he touched me, but I tried to ignore it. He was a king of magic and might and wealth, and I was a mortal princess, although here, I was merely Celeste, a tool for his needs.

We stepped through a crisscross of tunnels and passages until I was thoroughly lost. The air turned crisp, almost cold, and I heard water splashing against rock. The path sloped down, and above us, blue stones glowed, and fairies rushed ahead of us, rosy lights winking.

Cliffs surrounded us, and Zekiel came to a halt on the rocky shore, calling out, "Henri!"

A gnome poked his head out of a mere hole carved into the rock wall. He clasped his hands together and bowed when he saw us, his white beard almost touching the ground. "Zekiel, my king, I did not expect you today. How may I serve you?"

Zekiel gave a slight bow in return.

I speculated in confusion. What kind of king bowed to his subjects?

"Is the boat ready?"

"Aye," Henri nodded, "and the waters are quiet. It would be an honor to take you across myself."

"As you wish." Zekiel gestured to me. "This is Celeste. She is staying with us for a time."

"Lady Celeste." Henri bowed. "I'm Henri, the boat master, at your service."

"A pleasure to meet you," I said, uncertain if I should curtsy, for it felt silly to do so in leathers, and bowing seemed like a mockery rather than politeness.

Thankfully, Henri was already hastening away to the waters.

"Come," Zekiel said, hand at my back. "You'll enjoy the view."

The boat was perched on the shore, half in, half out of the water. It rocked back and forth while Zekiel and I climbed aboard and sat side by side, facing Henri.

Henri shouted, and two gnomes appeared to untie the boat and push it into the water. Henri took up the oars, and a moment later we were floating in the expanse of inky black water.

10

CELESTE

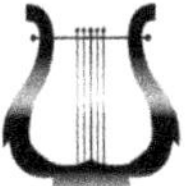

The gentle slap of the oars against the water was soothing, despite my need to shrink away from Zekiel's bulk. He sat beside me on the tiny craft, barely a hand's width between us, while Henri sat with his back to us, rowing.

I kept my gaze firmly pinned to the waters, examining the mushrooms that grew out of the walls and the bats that flew around us, nothing but a whirl of wings. Once, one dipped into the water near us, and I glimpsed a pointed, rat-like face and small red eyes. *Creepy*. Creatures of the night dwelled here, but that was to be expected in the kingdom of midnight.

My thoughts went to fairytales I'd read of an underground king and his hideous kingdom of death, destruction, and pain. From all accounts, the underworld was a place where the spirits of evil hovered, dwelling in a realm of death, eager to torture the living. Irradiance was not a place of pain or evil, and though it was dark, it sparkled with a beauty I never could have imagined.

The magical glow didn't merely come from the gems in the rock, but also from the water. Pale lights shone out, and I held onto the rim of the boat, watching the bats swoop and dive, catching something in their mouths. Were they eating fish? Something else?

Questions rose in my mind, but I dared not look at Zekiel. He was a king, half monster, and I was stuck with him for the next year, or at least until I escaped. He had more wealth than I could imagine, but what worried me was the strange allure of his presence that enticed me with more than mere curiosity.

In the palace, I'd been called odd, with unnatural desires. Was my attraction to a half-monster one of them? A burning within made my fingers tingle, and I tightened them into fists. Anxiety would get the better of me if I didn't distract myself. Keeping my gaze on the waters, I asked: "Where are we going?"

"This is Lake Calvania," Zekiel explained, his low voice rumbling. "It cuts through Irradiance. On the other side, we can reach the sacred gates. Again, it's better that you see once we arrive."

"I see," I mumbled, even though I didn't. With a quick glance at Henri, who didn't seem to be paying attention, I added, "When we reach the shore, will you tell me more about the task?"

Zekiel stiffened. "What do you know about fighting?"

My stomach twisted. "I wasn't trained to fight."

"Nor is there a need," Zekiel murmured.

I linked my fingers together, as his comment was far from reassuring. Where was he taking me? What would he force me to do?

The boat jarred against rock, shaking me from my thoughts as white butterflies fluttered above us, unsettled by our arrival.

Henri twisted around to face us. "Shall I wait?"

"No." Zekiel lightly stepped off the boat. "Come for us tomorrow evening."

Tomorrow? I almost choked at the idea of being gone for so long, but Zekiel held out his hand to assist me off the boat. I paused before extending my hand, but he'd retracted his claws. My skin tingled at his touch, firm and warm.

Once my feet were securely on solid ground again, I let go of him, hoping he wouldn't notice the quickening of my pulse. Henri floated away and Zekiel turned toward a long staircase that shot up into velvet shadows. Foreboding twisted in my belly as Zekiel walked toward those steps.

"We have entered the starlight realm. Down there, more of my people work." He gestured to a passageway leading deeper into the mountain, and even though it, too, was swallowed in darkness, a welcoming silver glitter came from the ceiling, making me want to go that way instead.

"And up here?"

"The sacred gates. Follow me."

Zekiel started up the intimidating staircase, which was nothing more than rough stone chipped into the mountainside. At times, the steps were large and deep, making it difficult to climb. I struggled behind Zekiel, glancing back occasionally with the wish that we were down below in the starlight realm.

The faint glistening of crystals lit the way, and soon, my thighs burned with exertion. Still, the stairs continued, and Zekiel did not pause once. I refused to look weak in front of him, so I panted and forced one foot in front of the other, trying not to look back to see how high we'd come.

The air shifted cooler, and a noise came, a pitch I found difficult to explain. It was a cross between a vibration or hum, a slight whine, not of pickaxes and workers singing, but something else.

At last, the stairs ended in blackness. I bent over, struggling to catch my breath, pinpricks of pain shooting up and down my legs as Zekiel moved forward into the shadows.

Words came from his lips, a chant in an ancient tongue. Unease prickled the hairs on my neck, and I shrank within myself, listening to the arcane words that flowed from his lips. The very air shivered and awoke, moving like a current under the power of his deep voice.

This was magic, and everything about it felt wrong.

I sensed a presence in the darkness with us, a malevolent force wishing us harm, and I wanted to beg him to stop. He'd summoned something awful, or awoken a terrible spirit, and I wished to be no part of it. Zekiel might be a king of wealth, but now I knew his secret. He was in league with something diabolical.

Suddenly, a sliver of light pierced the darkness and grew, brightening the space before me. My attention was drawn to a female spirit dressed in gray who hovered above us. Silver hair cascaded down her back, and her eyes glittered like sapphires, her mouth a pit of blackness.

I slapped my hands over my mouth to swallow down the scream inside. This was a ghost from another realm; what could Zekiel possibly want with her?

"Why have you summoned me?" the female asked, her voice low and dangerous.

A whimper escaped my throat.

"I've come to request access to the gates," Zekiel said.

"What have you brought me?" The specter lifted a white claw and pointed at me.

Zekiel moved swiftly, a strangled "No!" bursting from his lips as he positioned himself between me and the ghost. "Take what you need from me."

The specter hovered as if she would reject him, then

drew closer. "New blood is always best, but as you wish, King."

Ignoring the jab at his title, Zekiel held out his arm.

I drew in a sharp breath, horrified as I realized what he was about to do, or rather, what he would allow the specter to do to him. I felt dizzy as her lips latched around his wrist, and Zekiel stood like a marble statue while the specter sucked blood from him.

The bloodletting seemed to go on for an eternity, and the scent of iron hung heavy in the air. She was draining his lifeblood, and a fit of irrational anger rose within me. Zekiel was giving his blood willingly, but I hated the specter. She had no respect for a king and enjoyed what she took from him.

As she fed, her color changed from translucent to more human-like. The whiteness of her face became less pronounced, displaying the hollow of her throat and the pink tint of skin, tinged with blood. Bile rose in my throat, and I blinked away tears of horror as the specter finished her meal.

Zekiel turned his wrist upright and stanched the blood flow while the specter moved away. This time, instead of floating, she walked flat-footed, as though she had regained a bit of mortality again.

Flinging out her arms she shouted: "*O macrabre portos sacrendo.*"

The stone shuddered and light furled out, white and beautiful, a welcome relief from the evil that lurked in the shadows. Doors slid open, revealing a circular platform. Giant stone statues of four-legged beasts stood in a semi-circle, each one with a glowing door between their claws.

A sacred aura came from within that platform, along with the pulse of life, as though the light were alive, ebbing and flowing like life-giving blood. My legs threatened to give out as I stared at the mystic display in front of me. This was a sacred place, and an unnameable fear clawed up my throat to choke me.

I shouldn't be here. *We* shouldn't be here.

But Zekiel wasn't running away. His fingers closed around my upper arm, guiding me into the room with the glowing doors.

11

CELESTE

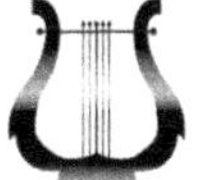

I attempted to swallow down my panic while we stood in front of the statues. They were carved from a sort of marble; not white but interwoven with various colors. Their eyes were jewels, and diamonds hung from their necks. Gold encased their feet, and each one cupped an item in their clawed hands, hovering just above the glowing doors.

I had the sixth sense that even though they appeared lifeless, the statues were alive, watching us through those glowing eyes. After all, I'd entered a realm of magic where anything was possible.

Zekiel strode to the first door without hesitation, fingers grazing the decorated doorknob, which was the head of a lion roaring, fangs glistening in the brilliance of white light. As he twisted it, the warning voice of the specter rang out. "Beware the time. Return in twenty-four hours or pay the price."

"I understand," Zekiel spat.

The feral anger in his tone both surprised and frightened me. Although I could not blame him for his attitude toward the specter, a burst of hot anger boiled within me as he thrust open the door and we stepped through the entrance.

A balmy breeze blew over my face, and daylight chased away the cloud of fear brought on by those sacred doors. I drew in a deep breath, inhaling honeysuckle and herbs.

We stood on a hilltop in a green meadow, where lush hills rose and fell around us. In the distance, a dark blur indicated buildings, perhaps a city. A blue sky stretched before us with gray clouds on the horizon, the omen of a coming storm. When I turned back around, the door was still there, but only a faint glimmer. I assumed the sacred gates were portals, and Zekiel had given his blood for access.

The knowledge left me feeling lightheaded and sick, though I recognized that if there was a time to run, it would be now. I scanned the area for cover as a shadow flew over our heads. My gaze was drawn to the cornflower blue sky, where a hawk stretched its wings, hunting.

"There you are," called a male voice.

Zekiel had already started down the hill toward none other than Ryder, who led two horses toward us. They weren't thick, solid horses like the ones that pulled carriages, but slimmer, with lean muscle, built for speed rather than labor.

Zekiel and Ryder exchanged a few low words, but as I neared, Ryder mounted up and rode down the hill while his hawk flew in lazy circles above us.

I paused in front of the horse, then held out my hand to the cinnamon-colored stallion. He sniffed my hand, then blew over it impatiently, drawing a smile from my lips. "He's beautiful," I murmured, cautiously stroking him since I'd be bitten twice by a horse. I loved the magnificent creatures and missed long afternoons spent riding my mare on the trails around the palace. It was the one time when everything melted away and what others thought about me did not matter.

"Do you ride?" Zekiel asked, patting the stallion's side.

"I do," I nodded.

He held out his hand, beckoning me closer. "Unfortunately, there was only time to procure one horse. This is better, though. At least I won't have to worry about you running away from me."

He tossed me on the horse's bare back and sprang up behind me. Powerful legs closed in on either side of me, and he pressed me against his chest, wrapping both arms around me to gather the reins.

With a click of his tongue, we were off, not into a full gallop, but a steady walk, as though we had all the time in the world.

A fact I knew was not true.

To distract myself from the fact that I was practically in his arms, I responded to his insulating comment. “What makes you think I’m going to run away?”

“This morning, you appeared unhappy about the deal we’d made, despite your eagerness the eve before. I warn you again, the contract is binding. Should you choose to default on it, you’ll find yourself back in that forest, and perhaps the trees will eat you after all.”

I stayed rigid, trying not to lean back into his warmth. “Trees don’t eat people.”

“I’d be careful with that assumption if I were you. Perhaps not in the mortal realm, but the limitations to magic are gone in that wood. You felt their menace. Trees will be whatever they wish to be.”

Then he leaned closer, until his mouth was right next to the shell of my ear as he whispered. “Beware of fairies. They are always treacherous, and their words mean nothing.”

I went cold all over, as if he had been privy to the conversation I’d had with Hada. How? Did he have magic that could hear all?

He didn’t give me time to respond as he urged the horse into a gallop, and all my focus went toward staying on the horse. Even though it was awkward to have his arms around me, he held me securely, ensuring I did not bounce around, or worse, fall.

We did not slow again until the dark mass came into focus–a city. Instead of continuing toward it,

Zekiel turned off the main path into a field, and we trotted toward a barn. As the horse slowed its speed, Zekiel relaxed behind me, arms loosening as he spoke. "We are in a country called Viridis. Have you heard of it?"

I thought back to the history books I'd leafed through in the palace library. "I have," I responded as Zekiel dismounted.

His large hands spanned my waist as he helped me down, and I instantly retreated, trying to put the horse between him and me.

"It's a peaceful country," I went on. "It does not fall under the reign of any kingdom. A group of monks dedicate their lives to prayer and working the land. In fact, they are known for their verdant gardens, and any kingdom that has tried to invade them has been struck down with plague and famine and death. Legend says the monks have a powerful deity who watches out for them."

My steps slowed to a stop as a realization crept over me. "No," I breathed. "You want me to steal from the monks. I can't! They will curse us."

Zekiel faced me, a snarl marring the perfection of his face. "You can and you will. Have you already forgotten our contract?"

Instead of backing down, I fought for the words to make him understand. "I'm not going back on my word, but the monks are powerful. If kings refuse to send armies to conquer them, what chance do we have?

They will find us and curse us, and whatever is wrong in your kingdom will get much worse."

Zekiel frowned. "What makes you think something is wrong with my kingdom?"

I waved my hands. "It's only a guess. You have wealth beyond what any kingdom could imagine. You could barter and trade for anything you want, and yet, you want me to steal."

Zekiel stepped toward me, his expression unreadable. "This is the most honest you've been with me."

He closed the distance between us until his chest was inches form my face and I was forced to look up at him. Those eyes; they were dark like a moon without light, and his horns, his claws, and that hand in a glove—how could I forget he was half-monster?

"I will tell you this once more," Zekiel whispered, his eyes trapping mine with the intensity of his gaze. "You willingly signed a blood contract. You must complete these four tasks or your life will be forfeit, and I don't believe you want me to hand you over to the specter to suck your blood. There are far more unsavory punishments for breaking your word, nay, for breaking a blood contract. Now, time is limited, so you will follow me and do as I command. Have I made myself quite clear?"

My heart pounded as his manly scent filled my nostrils. My legs felt weak, and my lips trembled, fumbling for a response. Again, my gaze was drawn to his lips, and an imprudent thought came to mind. *What if he took me? Pressed his lips against mine and gave me no chance to escape?*

When I didn't respond, Zekiel held up his hand, claws extended, and one by one, he retracted them before placing his fingers against my throat. My breath went shallow, but I didn't move, trapped under his spell. This was wrong, yet I *wanted* him.

"You forgot, Celeste, that I am inhuman. The laws that hold true in the mortal realm do not hold true for me. This might be Viridis, a lush land with all appearances of blessing and grace, but the monks are nothing more than its face, the kingdom instead run by shadow worshippers. You would be wrong to assume this is a kingdom of peace. Have you not heard the rumors? Of plague and death and famine, and that those who come here with ill intent disappear? You have. It's because this land is not what it seems."

His fingers left my neck, and although he had not squeezed or harmed me in any way, his touch lingered like a brand. "I…I understand," I gasped.

He did not move away. "Can I trust you, Celeste? So far, I've held up my end of the contract. You are clothed, well-fed, and safe, are you not? Will you uphold your end, or shall I be forced to return you to the forest, nay, even the queen, after we get out of this trouble?"

"You can trust me," I croaked. "But don't threaten me."

"It's not a threat, just the truth. Now come inside. Time is wasting and there is work to be done."

He led the horse toward the barn while I gingerly touched two fingers to my throat where his hand had been. He hadn't even applied pressure, but the very touch had been a warning. Even if I wanted to run from him, there was nowhere to go. An inkling wouldn't leave me alone. I was back in the mortal realm, so would the magical contract still hold?

The barn was clean inside, empty of animals. Hay was stacked against the walls, and to one side was a half table with two stools. Zekiel took the bridle off the horse and led it to a stall to rest and eat before going to the table. He slung off his bag and unrolled a scroll, then beckoned me over.

Tentatively, I sat down opposite him as he showed me the map. "If you know of Viridis, you know of the temple," he said, pointing to the drawing.

I nodded, offering some information of my own. "Yes, built into the mountainside where the hot springs flow."

"Correct."

I felt his eyes on me but focused mine on the map, trying not to beam at the fact that we were on even footing with this conversation. I shouldn't want to please him or have him think highly of me. He was, in fact, inhuman, likely wicked, and, despite his wealth, king of a very strange kingdom. I did not belong in his land, or with him for that matter.

"Your task is to enter the temple disguised as one of the worshippers," Zekiel explained. "The cloak should do the trick. I shall remain outside."

I drew in a sharp breath, my fanciful thoughts gone. "I go alone?"

"I cannot enter the temple, which is why you will go in my place."

Understanding dawned and I desperately wanted to ask why, but tension still hummed between us. I should have felt proud that an inhuman king needed a mere mortal to do his bidding, but it only made me want to run all the more. I'd done nothing hard in my life as a princess and what he asked of me was better fit for an outlaw, an assassin, or a hunter, someone who could easily blend in with a crowd and sneak in and out of places. Decidedly not me.

Bitter thoughts swarmed. I'd run away from the palace, but my freedoms with Zekiel were limited. Was it possible I'd gone from a terrible situation to something much worse?

"It's because you're inhuman, isn't it?" I blurted out. "If you need a mortal to do your bidding, why me? You already have mortals who work for you."

A raw look flashed through Zekiel's eyes, but he quickly recovered. "Very astute. It is because I need you, specifically. You are correct; as an inhuman, I may not stand in the sacred spaces without great harm."

I stilled, aware that through this conversation, I'd learned two very important things. The first was that he could not reach me if I were in a sacred place. My pulse quickened at the idea of escape, yet my chest swelled at the idea of being needed.

No one ever needed me.

I was a princess, a nuisance to my father, a burden to the crown. Zekiel offered me the chance to be useful. The idea of working for him was tempting, but wasn't stealing unforgivable?

Zekiel was still explaining. "This afternoon, we will continue on foot to the city in time for the evening service. You'll go to the temple and follow the monks as they climb to the top of the temple for the blessing. At the summit is a relic called the Lapis Solaris. You will procure the relic and bring it back to me, and then together, we shall return to the portal."

I stared at him, mouth half open. He made it sound so simple. "How will I steal the relic in the middle of a service? They'll notice."

Zekiel flexed his fingers, claws on display. "I will create a diversion for you to steal the Solaris. You'll need to be quick, focused."

I stared at the map, inwardly fuming. "How will I know what this relic looks like?"

One of Zekiel's claws tapped a symbol on the map.

"Surely, if you know of Viridis, you know of the sacred relic, a round orb that glows like the sun. It is only displayed during daylight and hidden away at night. During the morning and evening worship, the relic is on display. Inside the temple will be statues of the idols they worship. The one at the top of the temple, in the center, holds up Lapis Solaris for all the worshippers to see. There should be a staircase leading to the top for offerings."

"I understand."

"You are afraid, which is natural, but I will not let you fail."

I pressed my lips together before asking the question that hovered in my mind. "What if they catch me?"

"You will not need to fight here," Zekiel confirmed.

Despite his certainty, I couldn't shake the feeling that we were about to spring, purposefully, into a pit of vipers.

12

CELESTE

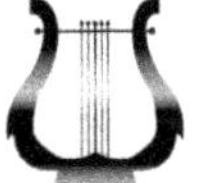

Waiting was monotonous, but at some point, a sense of determination washed over me. I was a princess. I could face any challenge life threw at me. Hadn't I escaped from the palace with the help of the huntress? Hadn't I sealed my fate by binding myself to an inhuman king? *The King of Hearts*. Surely, despite my fear, I could accomplish anything I set my mind to.

When Zekiel stood and pulled the cowl of his hood over his horned head, I quickly joined him. He cast a side-long glance at me. "Are you eager to begin?"

I frowned, keeping my negative thoughts to myself. "Eager isn't the word I'd use. Ready to get this over with."

He made some kind of sound in the back of his throat, a cross between a laugh and a grunt, then led the way out of the barn. We walked side by side down the dusty path that led to the city. It was unlike any land I'd ever seen, though I had little to go on, aside from scenes woven into tapestries or painted on walls. Despite my longing to escape the palace, I hadn't had the opportunity to travel to distant lands, and it was all I could do to keep from staring, wide-eyed, at the unfamiliar sights and sounds.

The cobblestone road stretched like a bed of gold, all roads pointing to the great mountain where the temple rose, an impressive building of stone with bright flashes of green growing between the stones. In fact, the entire city had a verdant tilt to it. Even though buildings lined the streets, behind them were stretches of land filled with gardens or orchards or vineyards, sloping away into rolling hills. It was an interesting design, for the buildings were the center of town and the gardens and farms were on the outskirts, making it vulnerable to any visiting kingdom.

Except no one came here for war; only for peace and to worship at the temple.

Zekiel nudged me as we approached the courtyard outside the temple. "The worshippers are lining up. You should join them. I'll wait here."

I swallowed hard, not wanting him to see my apprehension. With a nod, I forced my feet past the bubbling water fountain in the center of the courtyard to the smooth stone steps leading to the yawning entrance of the temple. Monks and—I assumed—citizens of the city were lined up, some wearing long robes, others in laymen wear, as though they'd just come from the fields and orchards for evening prayers.

Clasping my hands in front of me, I shuffled behind a long-robed monk. A slow chant began as we approached the steps where two monks stood on either side of the doorway.

"Hood off," one murmured as he handled me a candlestick.

Seeking to blend in, I removed the cowl from my head and took the offered candlestick. No one so much as looked at me as I followed the example of other worshippers and lit my candle from a nearby brazier.

The worshippers split in two. One group went left, and the other went right, up a curving stone staircase. Recalling Zekiel's instructions, I choose the left side at random and walked, one halting footstep in front of the other. It was a holy ceremony, meant to be taken seriously and slowly.

As we climbed, impatience tapped a rhythm in my heart as the worshippers chanted, and I tried not to rise on my tiptoes to see the summit. Suddenly, there it was: an orb that radiated light like the sun itself.

My breath caught as I stared at it. The holiness of the area, the chant of the worshippers, and a sense of awe captivated me. I moved on my own accord, feeling the strange need to sink to my knees and worship in the face of such beauty. A vibration filled my mind, as though the voice of the orb surrounded me, humming, and if I could just stand close enough, its presence would envelop me, the voice answering all the questions I pined to know the answer to.

Now I understood why many made the pilgrimage to worship at this shrine. The light gave me hope that I'd overcome my current situation. After all, I was in a sacred place where no inhuman could touch me, and if I pled my case, I was sure the monks would take me in and allow me to work at the temple until Zekiel had forgotten me.

Instinctively, my hand went to my neck where his fingers had touched, and my stomach somersaulted.

That's when the music began.

Familiar strains of a harp drifted from the entrance of the temple, and it was a moment before I realized the chanting had died away. All I heard was harp music. I'd come to a standstill, enchanted by the orb, but now, as I gazed about me, I noticed the worshippers had bowed their heads as if in prayer. Had I missed a queue?

Quickly, I bowed my own head and clasped my hands together, just as the person in front of me toppled over. My eyes went wide as one by one the entire assembly fell to the floor until I, alone, stood, listening to the lull of the harp, my eyes heavy. Sinking to my knees, I started to prostrate myself on the ground when a realization struck me.

This wasn't natural or normal. It must be the diversion Zekiel had promised he'd create. Either I lay down and pretended to sleep like the worshippers or...my gaze went to the orb. I should steal it. I balled up my fists, determined not to give in to the lure of that orb, the glistening light that called to me.

But it was irresistible.

As though under a spell, I moved among the prone worshippers until I stood directly in front of the statue. It was displayed on a dais, behind a rope, but I walked without thinking. I trotted up the stairs and leaned over the statue, fingers stretching toward the orb.

That hum echoed in my head again, filling me with a certainty that when I took it, all my wildest dreams would come true. When my fingers closed around it, a pain shot up my arm, as though I'd touched something hot. Hissing, I dumped the orb into the folds of my cloak, and out of the corner of my eyes, something black flickered. Black with red eyes. Was I being watched?

The urge to run came over me so strongly, it was difficult to resist. Hiding the orb, I pulled my cowl over my head and walked down the stairs, my breathing shallow. Ducking under the rope, I made my way around the prone bodies, waiting for a hand to lock around my ankle, for someone to shout for me to stop, but no one did.

Most of the candles had gone out when the worshippers had fallen, but one rolled against the tapestries, smoking the frayed edges. A deep, unsettling fear overcame my ability to stop and think. What had just happened was wrong—I'd given in to the darkness and stolen a powerful relic.

Beads of sweat formed on my brow as I moved faster, the open door of the temple calling to me. The voice of the harp was distant now, the bubbling of the water fountain louder, the voices of individuals in the courtyard swelling, waiting for the evening service to end.

As I stepped out, red hues covered the sky, a mark of the impending sunset. It was stunningly beautiful, and on any other day, I would have stopped to stare at the masterful artwork. Instead, I walked down the steps of the courtyard on trembling legs, arms heavy, my head bowed under the weight of what I'd done.

"Celeste."

I snapped my head up as Zekiel fell in stride beside me. He held a golden harp, which he tucked into a bag and slung over his back. Taking my arm, he guided me down an alleyway. "Let me see," he instructed.

Opening the cloak, I showed him the orb, gleaming in an inner pocket. To my surprise, Zekiel's arm tightened around my waist. "You succeeded," he whispered, awe in his deep tones.

It was only then that I dared look at him. His skin was almost as pale as his hair and an unnatural darkness glimmered in his eyes. Suddenly, I realized he was holding onto me for support. Something was terribly wrong.

"Zekiel?" I started, then recalled I wasn't supposed to care about him or his kingdom.

He leaned nearer, keeping his voice low. "Many things are about to happen, but don't scream and don't look back. We will calmly walk away."

Keeping his arm around me, he steered us out of the alleyway and down the road. We walked quickly, and I was tempted to glance back at the temple, but the weight of what I'd done, what I'd given into, sat heavily on my shoulders. I'd had a chance to escape, yet guilt plagued me, not for my own welfare, but for the fact that I'd taken the orb, the hope of these people. I was mortal; would I be cursed now?

An explosion shook the ground, and screams erupted from behind us. My hand flew to my lips, and I tried to turn back to see what had happened, but Zekiel's grip was iron. "Walk," he all but growled into my ear.

The scent of burning filled the air, and a bell rang out. Footsteps pounded past us, wails and cries bursting out, and a sense of numbness came over me. This was the work of Zekiel, and I was part of his horror.

13

CELESTE

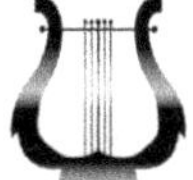

No one bothered us as we left the city and returned to the barn, where the horse waited for us. Wordlessly, we mounted up and fled under the cover of night. It was only on horseback that I dared look back at a plume of thick black smoke and flames leaping from the city.

"Did you have to burn it down?" I ask bitterly.

When Zekiel spoke, his voice was hoarse. "No one was intentionally harmed. It was only a diversion to ease our escape."

"How can you be so sure?" I snapped.

"I can't," he replied, voice so low, it was almost swept away under the thud of the horse's hooves.

A tense silence followed, and my chest hurt with the knowledge of what I'd done, the crime I'd committed because I had no self-control. Behind me, Zekiel's breath grew more labored and slowly, his grip weakened. His weight bore down on me as we continued, and my pulse quickened. What was wrong with him?

A pale light glimmered on a hilltop and obediently, the horse trotted toward it. It took me a moment to make out the faint outline of a door. The portal. We were back.

Fear clawed up my throat, but all thoughts of escape faded. Now was not the time. I needed to plan, needed a way to ensure I had food, money, and clothing before I fled. Thoughts of finding his treasury and stealing from it skipped through my mind, and then there was the trouble of escaping through a portal. That, I was sure, Hada could help with.

Zekiel tumbled off the horse and I slid with him, nearly tripping over my skirts. With a hoarse word and a pat, Zekiel sent the horse off downhill, then staggered to me. In the light, he appeared haggard, his skin almost translucent. Concern made me reach for him as his arm came down heavy across my shoulders.

"What's wrong with you?" I gasped as we hobbled toward the outline of the door.

"Magic," he grunted through gritted teeth.

Somehow, he managed to stand tall and lifted a hand, speaking the words of an arcane spell. Golden light blazed and the door opened. We lurched through and collapsed on the stone floor, panting. The light faded until we were left in pale gloom.

My legs were stiff as I pushed to my knees, but

Zekiel pulled me against him suddenly, his grip stronger, hands going to my neck. I gasped, immediately struggling for freedom as he unclasped my cloak.

The orb! That was all he wanted.

Free from his grip, I stumbled to my feet, anxious to be away from the statues and worried about the specter returning. Zekiel did not appear concerned about either. He cradled the cloak in his arms, those dark eyes studying me.

Wordlessly, I picked up the bag he'd been carrying and lifted my chin, determined not to show weakness in front of him.

"You did well," he said, his voice already stronger.

I hated the fact that my heart swelled under his praise.

Zekiel glided toward the exit. "Come. I will take you to the starlight realm, where you can rest."

"What about you?" I dared to ask as we descended.

"Me?"

"Yes, you. You were so pale and weak back there… on the other side."

"Ah." He glanced back at me ever so briefly. "Magic drained my strength."

I recalled the music of the harp, the worshippers sleeping, and the sudden urge I'd had to take the orb. It was clear he'd used music to cast a spell, but what sort of power did he have over me?

At the bottom of the staircase, I half-expected to see the gnome, Henri, waiting with the boat, but the waters were eerie and silent, making my skin crawl. Zekiel turned away from the lake and led me down a passageway.

At last, we paused in front of a door, which he pushed open. "This will be your room for the night. Rest."

I faced him, my throat thick with unsaid words. Briefly, I glanced at the cloak containing the orb, and my heart yearned to look at that light's glory again.

He lifted his good hand, and when I did not flinch away, he cupped my cheek. His touch was warm and comforting, and I leaned into it, surprised by how good it felt to be touched by him. His thumb caressed my cheek ever so gently before he withdrew, repeating his words from earlier. "You did well today."

My lips parted and I leaned closer, wanting him to touch me again, hating that my gaze flickered to his mouth and heat burned in my belly. I should not want to kiss this half-monster; I should want to escape. Yet, there was something about him that held me captive.

He turned away with a lingering, "Goodnight."

It was only when I shut the door that I realized I still held his harp.

14

ZEKIEL

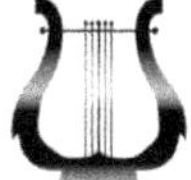

I left Celeste in the starlight realm and used my fingers to guide me down the short passage to my chambers. The rush of adrenaline from fleeing Viridis had left my body, leaving only pain and a terrible weakness in its wake. My vision blurred, my blood slowed, and dizziness made my head pound. It was the magic; I'd spent too much forcing the worshippers at the temple to sleep, but if I hadn't, she might have been caught, and our work would have been in vain.

Stumbling into the room, I collapsed, fist closing around the Lapis Solaris. I needed to sleep and rejuvenate, but my mind raced with concern. Taking the relic was a statement, and its importance would cause word to spread fast. Those who were wise might guess what was happening and realize that someone might be interested in all four relics. The next task would be much harder should those interested parties—immortals, I assumed—make themselves and their intentions known.

It would be best to make the next move now, tonight, if possible, but I could barely lift my head anymore. I must look terrible because Celeste's concern for me was potent and the care in her tone had piqued my interest.

Celeste.

I'd expected more trouble from her and anticipated that she'd run, hide, attempt something to try my patience. Instead, she'd performed her task quickly and admirably. Everything had gone well, a little too well if I were honest with myself. I admired her resilience, how she'd asked questions without backing down, as though she weren't afraid of me at all.

Curious.

I shouldn't have caressed her cheek, shouldn't have touched her like I cared. The unexplainable attraction I felt for her made it difficult to keep my hands to myself, but she hadn't rebuked me. If anything, she'd encouraged me.

My royal thief.

The plan was to use her and then…let her go. I *should* let her go. My kingdom was no place for a mortal princess. It was best if I put some distance between us, killed off what was budding and focused on securing safety and freedom for my kingdom.

15

CELESTE

Gems glowed like starlight around me, and it was easy to imagine I lay in a midnight sky under a cluster of silver light. That is, until I swayed gently in the hammock I'd fallen asleep in. An ache hovered in my limbs from the previous day's excursion, but when I pressed my palms to my heated cheeks, all I could think of was *him*.

I sat up, taking in what I'd missed while sleeping. It was a concave room, roughly hollowed into the stone. Gems embedded in the rock gave off a soft halo of light, and aside from the hammock and a basin of water, the room was empty.

I washed as best I could, still feeling some of the grit and dust from the road, but I had no other clothes to change into. When a soft knock came at the door, my heart leaped.

Zekiel.

Running my hands over my wrinkled clothes, I opened the door and swallowed down sharp disappointment.

Yosa stood on the other side, her emerald eyes sparkling as she studied me. She gave an intoxicating chuckle. "I wondered if you'd be awake. We meet again."

My brow furrowed. "Yosa, correct?"

"You remembered!" Yosa grinned broadly and hooked her arm through mine. "I promised Zekiel I'd take good care of you while you're here in the starlight realm. I'd be honored to show you around."

"Oh," I breathed, realizing I didn't have much choice.

I strained to pull the door shut before she whisked me away, trying to shake off the disappointment that Zekiel hadn't come for me instead. Why should he? He was king, after all, and I'd just stolen a precious relic for him. It was likely he was off studying it.

Still, Yosa seemed inclined to talk, and my lonely heart wanted a friend, a place to belong. Besides, I knew little about Irradiance and would feel lucky if she gave me valuable information, especially since down here—to my relief—no fairies presented themselves to annoy me.

"What, exactly, do you do here?" I asked.

"Oh, me?" Yosa laughed. "I'm in charge of gem production."

My eyebrows lifted. *Gems? Did she know where the trea-*

sury was? “I’m afraid I know nothing about gem production, but it is beautiful down here.”

“Isn’t it? I fell in love with the caverns when I first arrived. I can’t imagine any other life.”

“What did you do before you lived here?” I asked, grasping for more clues about her background.

“Oh. That.” Yosa wrinkled her nose and waved her hand. “A word of advice, Celeste, since you’re new here. The past is the past, often an ugly, awful scar on our histories before Zekiel took us in. I’m assuming the same could be said for you, and you wouldn’t dare discuss your life before…well…here. Am I right?”

I shivered. “You are, but…”

Yosa cut me off. “All you need to know is it was terrible, and now I’m here and happy, with a purpose. Now, I admit I am curious about you and your past, but I’ve learned that there are some things that needn’t be discussed.”

I chewed my lower lip, still fishing for information. “How long have you been here?”

“Oh, the better part of a decade, maybe two? Who knows. I lost count.”

I gave her a side-long look. “But you don’t seem… well…you appear quite young.”

“Bless you for saying that. I’ve seen four decades at least. It’s generous of someone young and beautiful like you to say such a thing about me.”

My fingers went to my short hair. It was kind of her to compliment me, but I’d never felt beautiful. “I’m not that young," I murmured, for I'd almost seen three decades.

Yosa rushed on, her words tumbling over each other in their haste to escape her mouth. "I already know I'm going to enjoy your company, a welcome reprieve from the gnomes. Don't take that the wrong way, though. Gnomes are wonderful and some of the hardest workers I've ever met."

"What about the man called Ryder?"

"Oh. Him." Yosa snorted. "He's never around anyway, and, between you and I, not the best sort of company. He's a king's man through and through."

I wondered what that meant but didn't press for further details as Yosa took a sharp turn into a small room. The scent of peppermint hovered, and silver glitter lit up the enclosure.

"We rarely light fires down here, since there's nowhere for the smoke to go," Yosa explained, letting go of me. "We do keep some food, though. What do you want for breakfast?"

"Uh..." I murmured, shrugging.

Yosa moved around the room with purpose, opening shelves and pulling out items. "We all work in shifts, so we come and go as we please. There's a bit of bread, cheese, oh, and a treat! Some smoked salmon. I dare say, you'll need your strength."

Within seconds, she spun and handed me a pocket of bread. I tentatively bit into it, and the flavors of smoky fish, sharp cheese, and yeasty bread burst in my mouth. It wasn't rich, but it was hearty and delicious.

Yosa bit into her own pocket of food, swallowing down the bite as she led the way out of the room. "Now this is my favorite part."

I'd been staring guiltily at the trail of crumbs we left behind on the stones, but now I looked up. The path ended at an overlook. Yosa propped a hip on the stones and spread her arms, indicating the expanse below as she took another bite. I stood shock still, suddenly understanding why it was called the starlight realm.

Diamonds glittered above us, the white light shining like stars over the workers below. Low murmurs and cheerful whispers floated to my ears. In the past, I never would have called darkness beautiful, nor the bleak duskiness of a cave enchanting. Yet, once again, I found myself in awe of Zekiel's kingdom.

Irradiance was everything. Longing made my heart ache, though I didn't know what it was I wanted. Yosa had mentioned purpose, and I didn't know mine. All I had was a contract and the promise of a new life once I fulfilled it.

"What are they doing?" I asked.

Gnomes sorted gems, another group delivered different ones to each station, and others took them away in sacks or wheelbarrows. It was a dance of sorts. Everything had its place and everyone had a task. Even odder, everyone seemed happy about it.

Yosa leaned over the overlook, her voice animated.

"After the gems are mined, they are brought down here, unrefined. Lumps of rock cling to them along with gem dust, so they are purified. Once clean, we take care of sorting them, identifying their value, and determining where each gem goes. Some are melted down, others crafted into fine jewelry, and still others go to the treasury. Gems are used for trade or decoration. I oversee it all and determine the worth, value, and placement of each gem according to the needs of the kingdom. My favorite task is deciding what to do with the unrefined ones."

The passion in her tone was impossible to miss, and her eyes gleamed as she stared across the expanse at her work.

That ache inside me swelled. Even with my lofty status as a princess, my life had felt aimless and hollow. I knew I was to take my place as a royal, with a marriage that would benefit two kingdoms and children who would grow up to rule. All of that had been snatched away and I'd been given the unique chance to choose my destiny; at least, once Zekiel was finished with me.

I had a choice in who I'd become, what I wanted to do, where I wanted to go, and how I wanted to live. If only I found something that gave me half as much joy as gems gave Yosa.

Her voice dropped to a low, reverent tone. "You know, jewels aren't simply for jewelry. Everyone assumes that's what they are for, but they have other uses. They can be inlaid in weapons, carved into statues, put into food, crafted into glassware, and much more. I enjoy decorating the castle with them, but my favorite is the crystal forest. I cultivated it with gemstones until they grew on their own. They are breathtaking. I'm most proud of my work there."

I'd never heard of such a thing. "I'd like to see your crystal forest, but what kind of jewels do you keep in the treasury?"

"Oh, only the rarest ones go there. Once, we found a diamond as big as my head." Yosa laughed. "Another time, a set of pearls that shone like moonlight. There are so many rare and varied treasures here, but the discovery is what I enjoy. Actually, that leads me to why you're here."

My eyes went wide as I finished my breakfast and my heart pounded. Did she, too, know of the deal I'd made with Hada? "Me? Why?"

Yosa squeezed my arm. "He didn't tell you, did he? It's payment, of course. All he told me was that you're retrieving items for him, so you'll need to be paid for it, and you can choose."

My heart squeezed as I recalled the clause in the contract about payment. When Yosa first came to Irradiance, had she, too, been under the confines of a contract? If so, when it ended, she'd clearly chosen to stay in Zekiel's kingdom.

A memory of his pale skin, those dark, unreadable eyes, and the toll magic had taken on him made me yearn to see him again. According to Yosa, he was alive. He had endured. I wanted to know what was wrong in his perfect kingdom, but Yosa did not seem the person to ask, even though I liked her.

"Ah, there you are," Yosa said gently. "I lost you for a moment. If you're ready, we'll go down and I'll help you choose a fair payment."

16

ZEKIEL

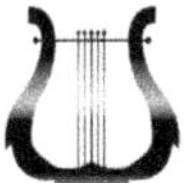

The Lapis Solaris pulsed in my hands, golden light beaming as though it were alive. It was warm to the touch and when I held it up to the light, liquid gold stirred inside. I had no doubt it was alive, but there were no instructions on how to use it to achieve my purposes.

Standing in the chamber of portals, I held the relic over each basin, waiting, watching, hopeful for a change.

Nothing happened.

It was only the first test. I had three others in mind, yet as I held the relic, a heat surged up my bad arm, numbing the pain.

It was rather pleasant, honestly. So far, the strings from the harp eased my pain, but it would be foolish to carry around a precious relic, one others would be eager to steal.

A quiet step alerted me of a presence, and I turned to the entrance, waving my hand to usher in Ryder. "How are the borders?"

"My hunters report foul beasts skulking near the southern borders, giant hell dogs. They can't get in, not yet, and if they do, my hunters will hold them off. If she sends armies, though, what little magic we possess will not be enough."

Outwardly, I stayed calm.

It was true. The legend said all four of the relics were supposed to work together, and I suspected that Celeste might be the key. Except using her to test the relics wasn't part of our bargain, and part of me wanted to protect her. Unfortunately, she was but one mortal, and the kingdom was at stake. I shouldn't hold back in any way.

"This is all a gamble," I said. "There are still limitations to what the sorceress can do, but as my power weakens, hers grows stronger. This will give us some time, but we should move on to the next location before others become wise to what we are doing."

"My lord." Ryder bowed, then hesitated. "What of the princess?"

My jaw went tight. "What of her?"

"Don't you think there's more to her than meets the eye? Have you tried. . ." He trailed off, letting the thought hang between us.

I stilled. "I will try everything. I will not stop until the sorceress is defeated, you have my word."

Ryder nodded, a grim smile coming to his lips before he slipped away. The only words that echoed in my mind was the warning from Oren: *Don't let the haze of revenge make you lose sight of what's important.*

17

CELESTE

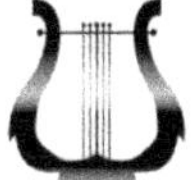

Seven days passed in the starlight realm, and I spent my days working with Yosa, enchanted by the glistening gems. I'd never worked a day in my life, and I assumed it would be difficult and I'd wish myself elsewhere. Instead, I had a sense of accomplishment and pride as I assisted Yosa. She sparkled with intelligence, had a kind word for everyone, was full of stories, and constantly laughed.

She showed me how to use a fine brush to clean dust and dirt off the gems so they gleamed brightly. I learned how to sort by weight and shine level and color, but I found the long, slim crystals set aside for the forest most fascinating. Yosa assured me that with the proper care, they would grow to be the size of trees, a feat that seemed impossible.

One thought was constantly with me, and despite throwing myself into work, I couldn't forget about him.

The more time that passed, the more my heart sank. I pined for fresh air and sunlight, and even though I had a year of service to go, I hoped he'd return soon for my next task. I tried not to fret about it—wasn't I supposed to hate him?

One morning, while I washed and waited for Yosa to knock on my door, my gaze was drawn to the bag I'd left in a corner. Zekiel's bag. Of course; why hadn't I considered looking inside it for clues? Excitement made my fingers shake, and even though I was alone, I glanced over my shoulder for watching eyes. Thankfully, no fairies dwelled underground.

Lifting the edges of the bag, I uncovered the harp. The golden edges gleamed in the low light, and I tentatively traced my fingers over the gilded edges. It was a beautiful piece of craftsmanship, leaving me wondering if it had been welded of pure gold. It wasn't heavy when I lifted it. The strings vibrated, begging me to touch them, and when I did, a melody rang out, as true and clear as a siren's call.

Emotion swelled thick as I plucked another note. Suddenly, there was a knock on the door.

Yosa.

I hastily recovered the harp and threw open the door. Yosa was not on the other side.

Instead, my heart flipped as I gazed up at Zekiel.

He was magnificent, his white hair hanging loose, his black horns shining, a dusting of gem dust covering his broad shoulders. Once again, his lavender shirt was open, displaying the rippling muscles of his torso. He was hale and healthy, tall and powerful, and a fluttering began in my lower belly.

Part of me was tempted to slam the door shut and lean against it to give myself time to recover my tongue. Smoky gray eyes studied me, but the hardness of his marble-like face did not waver. *What was he thinking?*

"Celeste," he said.

The sound of my name on his lips broke the spell, and a flash of anger returned. "You're back. Why did you leave me down here? Where did you go?"

His jaw worked, and he glided past me into the room, searching until his gaze landed on his bag. Taking out the harp, he studied it before returning his attention to me. "I had business."

I crossed my arms, an ache worming its way through my body. "And now you've returned for your harp?"

He brushed his fingers over the strings and again came that high sound, a call. "Technically it's a lyre. The rounded edges make it easier to carry and play, much easier than my other harps."

I raised an eyebrow, curiosity overcoming anger. "How many harps do you have?"

"Many. Do you enjoy music?"

Something inside of me softened. "I do. I used to play when I was younger, but my father believed it was a waste of my skills."

Zekiel's eyes clouded. "That is a shame. He was unaware of the power of music."

I swallowed hard, recalling what had happened at the temple. "It was you in Viridis, wasn't it? You used the magic of the harp to make the worshippers fall asleep."

He nodded. "Yes. I placed them under a spell."

"And the explosion. It was a diversion created by the other mortals you work with?"

His voice dropped and he took a step nearer. "It was. If the monks noticed the relic was gone right away, we never would have escaped so easily."

I shuddered. "Is every task going to be like that?"

"Yes, and no. Each task is unique. Enough about that; I did not come to discuss the next task."

"Then why did you come?" I asked, hoping for another reason.

He lifted the harp. "To return this to my collection."

I blinked, wishing he'd come to see me specifically. The night we'd returned, something had passed between us, and I was certain it wasn't just my imagination. He'd cupped my cheek, so gentle, and I wanted to feel that connection again.

"You are well?" Zekiel asked, those gray eyes studying me. "Have you decided on payment?"

My mind flashed to the treasury and the deal I'd made with Hada. "I am well. I enjoy working with the gems and with Yosa, but I do miss the sunshine. Might I return above with you?"

A darkness passed over him, like winged shadows of night. "You are safer down here."

I lifted my chin. "That may be true, but you promised me food, shelter, and clothes. I've been wearing the same clothes for seven days, I'd like a bath, and I'd like some sunshine. Is that too much to ask or am I your prisoner down here?"

A wry smile came to his lips. "You are not my prisoner. Come, then, but you may only go where I tell you. Oh, and do not speak to the walls."

"Because they'll try to eat me, like the trees?"

Zekiel smirked. "Something like that."

I followed him out of the bedchamber, a mix of thoughts dancing in my mind as we made our way back to the lake. This time, Zekiel rowed us across, and I watched him out of the corner of my eye, both irritated and enchanted by the movement of his muscles as he rowed.

This wanting, this *longing*, for him wasn't something I'd experienced before. Loathing filled me as I tried to fight off my attraction for a half-monster. I'd fallen into a world with rules I knew nothing about. He was inhuman, I was human, but regardless, he was a king. A king without a crown. A king who stole relics and caused chaos in other lands. I should despise him.

I didn't.

18

CELESTE

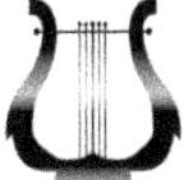

Zekiel left me at the pool I'd originally woken up in.

Stripping off my filthy clothes, I submerged myself in the heated waters, scrubbing until my skin hurt and the water shone with gem dust. It was a relief to fully submerge myself instead of pouring water over my head.

While I was drying off, the whir of wings came and a small army of fairies flew into the cavern, carrying a dark green dress. They draped it on the stone beach and peered at me expectantly.

My shoulders went stiff. "Thank you," I murmured politely. "Did Zekiel send this?"

Hada's rosy light shone out as she flittered around me. "Nonsense. We made it for you to celebrate your return to the land above, and the deal you made with us."

Bile churned in my belly because I'd purposefully forgotten about the deal. "I see," I said, recalling Zekiel's words about the treachery of fairies. I wished I'd had the presence of mind to speak with Yosa. She was the one individual I trusted in the realm, because she expected nothing from me. "I need to discuss payment with Zekiel. Do you know where I might find him?"

A titter went up, as though the fairies thought my question funny. Hada twirled in the air, waving them away. One by one, the tiny army made their way out, some skipping through the pool, flinging drops of water at my dry feet. I tried to ignore their mischievousness, but irritation rose until I was alone with Hada.

She floated over the dress, brushing at the shiny material.

"If you hurry, you'll find Zekiel in the greenhouse, tending to the plants. Now, we made you a lovely dress to warm against winter's chill. What have you found out about the jewel?"

"Nothing yet, but I am due payment. When I meet with Zekiel, I'll ask him about the treasury."

Hada made a popping sound with her lips. "You're quite direct, aren't you? Of course, I know where the treasury is. The problem is accessing it."

Curious. "It is sealed by magic?"

"A question not worth asking. Everything here is

bound by threads of magic. The question you should be asking yourself is why you are here."

I watched her, wondering whether I should consider her a friend or foe. "It is a question I haven't received a satisfactory answer to, but you know the answer, don't you?"

Hada cackled and twirled. "Get dressed, why don't you, and return to the room where you signed that contract of doom. There's an exit there. Follow the path that leads to the greenhouse. I'll find you later to see how you fared."

With a sprinkle of fairy dust across the stones, she flitted away.

As soon as I was alone, I slipped the dress over my head, dried my hair, and moved to the looking glass. The fairies had chosen well; the dark green complimented my skin tone and the cut of the dress molded perfectly to my body, tapering at the waist and flaring out slightly. My only complaint was that it dipped low in the front, exposing the swells of my breasts. I didn't want Zekiel to think I sought him out to seduce him, but perhaps it wouldn't hurt.

A low surge of desire passed through me. *Was it so wrong to want to be held, loved, kissed?*

Discarding that dangerous idea, I tugged on the matching slippers and left the bath chamber, fingers trailing against the cool rock. It was quiet, dark, and damp down there. It had only been seven days without true daylight, yet a wistfulness came over me, a sweet desire to walk under the light of the sun and feel the warmth of the rays on my upturned face.

The cold seeped into my bones, and a strange sensation made my skin prickles, as though I were being watched. Discomfort rose and I quickened my pace, trying to persuade myself it was only the oddity of a magical place. I couldn't shake the presence I felt, as though something foul wished me harm.

A low growl came, deep and guttural. I felt the fury of it like a slap to the face. Flinching away from the wall, I dashed up the stairs and around the corner. I did not stop running until I was in the room where I'd signed the contract. I slammed the door shut and leaned against it, chest heaving.

Luckily, the room was empty, and as I caught my breath, it occurred to me that I hadn't considered my surroundings. I imagined I was somewhere underground, although there appeared to be different levels to it. In Irradiance, I felt safe, surrounded by the gnomes and Yosa. The darkness, instead of being something to fear, was beautiful, with gems and dust sparkling like a sea full of starlight.

Up here, though, something unnerved me, and I hadn't considered why until now.

It was the silence and the lack of people.

So far, I'd seen Zekiel, Ryder, Yosa, the gnome Petra —who didn't seem like a personal maid after all—and the other gnome, Hinko, who'd brought me food my first night in the castle. Aside from fairies, who else dwelled in this quiet kingdom?

A kingdom should have a court; a king needed escorts, an army, advisors and servants. Where were all the people? If Zekiel had all those, they were well hidden.

I listened a beat longer, but the growl did not come again. Still, ice filled my veins as I cross the room to the doors outside. A wool cloak lay over the back of a chair, and remembering that it was late winter, I put it on and stepped outside.

Sunlight beamed down on my head like a goddess proud of her creation, and my jaw dropped in awe. I stood on a balcony with velvet moss and trailing vines growing along the railing. A set of three stairs led down to a stone path. A lush lawn stretched to the iron gates of the castle, and beyond that, rolling hills hidden by broad trees offered only a peek at the rich landscape.

Green shoots already covered the ground, and the trees budded with pink and white flowers in anticipation of an early spring. Rows of green plants grew on the rolling hills, and the sound of water came from beyond. All this time, I assumed I was in a cavern in a barren land, but when I gazed up, the wicked spirals of a castle gazed back down at me. Zekiel was rich in gems and land, too.

Who was he? An immortal king who lived beneath the crust of the Earth who needs a mortal princess to do his bidding. Why? A mystery lay here, and I longed to discover it.

Once I regained some control over my astonishment, I left the balcony and started down the paved path. Canary yellow and peacock blue flowers were cloistered near the walkway, their vibrant faces upturned to the light. They made the gardens in the palace pale in comparison.

A glimmer caught my eye, and I leaned closer to the upturned dirt. What I'd mistaken for crystal-like dewdrops were jewels: crimson rubies, midnight blue sapphires and diamonds sparkled in the flower beds. My fingers ached to touch them, but I snatched my hand back. Was it a trick? Who would leave gems lying on the ground where anyone could pick them up?

Perhaps it was a temptation meant to force me into yet another contract. A fairytale danced through my memory, of people who were stolen and tricked into eating and drinking faerie food, which made it impossible for them to return to the world of mortals. The fated tale was a reminder that I needed to watch what I took for myself. Stealing from the gardens might bring on a penalty, although a bubble of anxiety welled up at the reminder of the relic I'd stolen from the monks.

The path was longer than I expected, and I crossed a bridge spanning a pond. A thin layer of ice floated on top, broken up by lily pads. Deep croaks rang out as frogs splashed in the water, my shadow frightening them as I peered down.

Turtles sunbathed on rocks while bright-colored fish as big as my forearm swam back and forth. Birdsong echoed in the distance and a light breeze blew, bringing the fragrant scent of herbs to my nose.

It was peaceful and quiet, almost too quiet, but my heart warmed. Why had Zekiel wanted me to stay in Irradiance when this lovely land lay here? If I asked, would he allow me to stay in the gardens under the widespread blue sky and warm rays of golden sunlight? I'd have to persuade him. Then, the thought hit me: what did it matter? I intended on escaping, didn't I?

A crystal dome winked beyond a clump of trees. As the foliage opened, a building made of glass rose in front of me. A wheelbarrow full of dirt sat outside it, alongside pots, some filled with plants, others empty.

Greenery hung over the entrance, and a floral fragrance mixed with a hint of herbal spice filled the air as I stepped across the threshold. Vines and dried flowers hung from the glass ceiling, and rows of potted plants lay in front of me, mostly green with plumes of bright colors sprinkled throughout.

At the very end of the greenhouse was a multi-tiered water fountain, carved from crystal. It contained the statue of a woman, half human, half fish, pouring a shell of water onto the rocks. The sound of water lent a peaceful cadence to the greenhouse, along with the faint sound of clippings.

I took a step, and something curled around my

ankle and yanked. I shrieked as a green garden snake made its way up my leg.

No, it wasn't a snake, but a vine with a thick, snake-like head.

I kicked, trying to dislodge it as something brushed against my head. I slapped at it with my hand, which was a mistake, for more greenery from the ceiling wrapped around my wrist. What madness was this that the plants would come alive? Tugging and kicking, I struggled for freedom.

Feast. Feast, came a hiss, the meaning of the words clear.

Rivers of green vines swarmed toward me, hauling me up until I hung by my arms, suspended from the ceiling. My efforts were in vain as vines anchored my feet, spreading them apart until I thought I'd split. My chest burned with panic as I struggled, but the vines held firm.

A sudden memory broke through the haze of panic, a reminder of the night Queen Vivian had entered my room, ripping off the covers. Guards had held me down while she questioned me, using her knife to split open my skin, as though I were some prisoner, some traitor to the crown. She'd dared to interrogate me about the death of my father, as if it were my fault, not hers.

She'd left me with bloody legs and arms but no scars, as though she knew how to do just enough damage to cause pain but not deep scars. That's when I began to fear her, and shortly after, the huntress helped me escape.

A ripping sound brought me back to the present, and a sinking sensation of hopelessness overcame me. Thorns shredded my skirts, and a sharp pain came as they burrowed under my skin. I screamed, trapped in their grasp, suspended in midair while the snake-like heads of the vines burrowed in my skin, sucking my blood.

White hot flares of pain laced up my arms and legs and I thrashed helplessly, causing the cloak to fall off my shoulders. I could have sworn I heard tiny voices laughing as the veins tightened around my chest and throat, choking off my breath. It was like I was back in the forest, where plants had a mind of their own and a thirst for blood. Why did everything want to eat me?

"Enough!" roared a voice, and everything ceased.

19

CELESTE

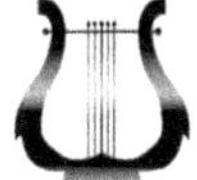

The veins released me, and I fell, but strong arms caught me, pressing me against warm, bare skin.

Zekiel.

My heart soared and sank all at once.

Cradling me in his arms, he lay me down on a work-table, frowning as he stood, shirtless, over me. In the daylight, he was resplendent, a shine of sweat covering his bronze skin, his moon-colored hair tied at the nape of his neck. He was all muscle, hard lines, and angles, with trousers that sat dangerously low on his hips. Despite his lack of a shirt, he still wore one black glove that ended just below the bend of his elbow.

An intense frown covered his face as he brushed his hand over my shredded skirt, baring my thighs. I tried to move my legs together, aware the fairies had given me no small clothes and once again, I was practically naked in front of him.

"Lie back," he instructed with a hand on my shoulder.

A low thrum of heat passed through my lower belly as I obeyed. Propping myself up with my elbows, I watched as he studied the thorns sticking out of my legs as though I were a pin cushion.

"This will hurt," he said matter-of-factly, and one by one, he pulled the thorns free, tossing them onto the ground.

I bit my tongue, holding my whimpers until he was done. Blood rolled down my legs, and I forced my gaze away, ashamed of what had happened to me.

Zekiel stepped away to dip a cloth in water, cleansing my wounds with surprising gentleness. When he finished, he placed a hand on my thigh, keeping me pinned down as his gray eyes sought mine. "What are you doing here?"

My nostrils flared. His tone of voice indicated I was to blame for what had just happened. "I came to find you, to speak about payment for the thieving I did for you," I spat.

His expression remained stoic, but he removed his hand from my thigh. Breathing hard, I forced myself to keep my gaze trained on his face and not linger on his perfect abs. A half-monster like him did not deserve to have a well-toned body like that. Worse, every time I saw more of his flesh, a lust burned within, to be touched, desired, and wanted by this haunted king.

I wanted to run my fingers down his chest, touch

him, taste him, watch the dark pools of his eyes shift from cold distance to warmth. I recalled the way his hand felt against my cheek, the brush of his thumb against my skin, the delicate sensations that rushed through me. What'd learned thus far in my life had taught me that a princess shouldn't have such wanton desires, especially not for an inhuman. My place was quiet obedience, to be seen and not heard, to birth heirs and nothing more, but what was the use in lying to myself? What little I knew about him intrigued me, and I wanted *him*.

"Everything in my kingdom endeavors to protect me," Zekiel explained, retrieving a vial from a shelf.

Uncorking it, he sprinkled the ingredients over my legs, perched a hip on the table, and started rubbing in the liquid. The pain from the bite of the thorns faded, leaving only a pleasant tingling. I shifted uncomfortably because his hands against my legs only increased my budding desires. My breath turned shallow, and I turned my face away, aware that beneath what remained of my shredded skirt, I was wet. I only prayed Zekiel didn't notice my arousal.

He went on talking, his voice low and steady. "The vines sensed an intruder and attacked. If I'd known you were coming, I would have been prepared."

"I thought I would be safe here," I said tightly.

Zekiel finished with my legs and faced me. To my surprise, a deep sorrow lurked in the depths of his gaze. "You are only safe from the terrors of your former life. Here, there are others who wish me and my kingdom harm. I do what I can to protect those under my care. In truth, you should have stayed below in Irradiance. That is where you are safest." His gaze flickered to my chest. "May I?"

My mouth went dry, until I realized he wasn't propositioning me, but pointing to the scratches. I nodded mutely as I sat up. Zekiel's hands went to the sleeves of the dress, which he let slip down my shoulders. Gently with his good hand, he rubbed the salves over my neck, fingers dipping lower with each move. I closed my eyes, giving in to the fever of heat that coiled deep in my belly, sending ripples of delight through me.

I shouldn't enjoy his caress, his fingers against my bare skin, chasing away the pain, leaving only pleasure. A soft sigh came, and I could not tell whether it was from my lips or his, but I keenly felt his absence as he moved away.

When I opened my eyes, he held the cloak. Returning to my side, he brought it around my shoulders and clasped it around my neck, standing so near, I could have turned my face and kissed the inside of his wrist. Instead, I studied his face, suddenly emboldened by his presence. He did not move away. Instead, his hands rested on the clasp of the cloak as though he, too, were under some spell.

A desire to touch him overcame me, and heat coiled deep in my belly. Hesitantly, I lifted a hand and pressed it against his, holding him near me. "What's wrong, Zekiel, with your kingdom? By all appearances, it's perfect, but it's not, is it? Otherwise, you wouldn't need me."

"True," he murmured, his gaze holding mine. His voice was low and sensual, sending shivers up my veins. "But I dare not tell you. Just know that your actions help me."

Suddenly it all came rushing back: my reason for seeking him out, the desire to escape, to leave. My gaze flickered to his tempting lips, and my throat went tight. I wanted to taste him, but it would be more reasonable to flee.

"I came to ask for payment," I said, still enthralled by his gaze. The depths of his eyes were like deep water, always shifting and changing under the light.

"What do you desire?"

You. The devilish thought popped into my mind before I could stop it. "I was hoping I might be able to pick something from the treasury."

There. I'd broken the spell, for his lip curled almost into a snarl. I glimpsed wicked sharp teeth that should have made my bones shiver.

"The treasury is off limits. You may pick your payment from Irradiance. Perhaps a handful of gems?"

I wanted gems, but I also wanted something else. "What would you ask for if you were in my place?"

His hand shifted lower on my chest, pressing against my heart and hovering there. Tilting his head, he studied me, his thighs pressing against my knees. "There is more you want."

My heart skipped a beat. "Yes," I breathed, overwhelmed by the dizzying sense of intense longing.

Holding my gaze, he leaned closer, his lips almost touching mine. "*This* is what you want."

His words came out as a statement, as though he read my mind, but he did not close the distance and kiss me. He hovered right there, waiting for permission. Closing my eyes, I tilted my face and leaned forward. Only an inch of space separated us, and my lips brushed his, warm and smooth and intoxicating. The headiness of his masculine scent surrounded me, only increasing my arousal as he kissed me back with more gentleness than I imagined possible.

I parted my legs, pressing my knees on either side of his hips, unable to explain what I wanted but hoping, just by my actions, he could tell. A strangled sound came from his throat and one arm wrapped around my back, holding me securely as he undid the clasp of the cloak, letting it fall free.

Cool air wrapped around my heated body as he tilted me back, his hand on my heart shifting lower, fingertips dancing over the swells of my breasts and dipping into my dress. His tongue brushed the seam of my lips, and I opened my mouth, welcoming his taste, his touch, his scent. His hand palmed my breasts, fingers squeezing my nipple, electing breathy moans from my lips.

Oh, but he kissed me, long, hard, as though he meant it, awakening passion, drawing me out of my shell, making me his. His teeth nipped at my lips and suddenly, I was lying down again. He moved between my legs, brushing away the shredded remains of my skirt, baring me, opening me completely to him.

He groaned. "This is what you want?"

I realized he was asking because I'd been quite clear that night in telling him I didn't want to be his whore. However, this didn't feel like sex for the sake of sex. It felt real, deeper, as though there was an authentic connection between us.

"Yes," I said, arching my back, because now I was in the throes, and what had begun could not be stopped, nor did I want it to end.

"Your taste, your scent, is delectable," he murmured.

Using one hand, he bent my legs, spreading them wider before he spread my lips, revealing my hooded clit, my arousal clear. One finger moved up, rubbing gently as I arched, my breath hissing out as threads of passion consumed me. When I opened my eyes, Zekiel stood between my legs, stroking me to pleasure and studying the expressions on my face.

Something about the look on his face, the way he drank me in, felt intrusive, and I squirmed as he held me down. Delicious tension swayed between us, and my chest heaved, bare breasts on display, my nipples hard and aching as he stroked me again. I jumped, a fire of passion spreading, tingling sensations shooting up and down my veins. Once more he repeated the caress, and I was gone over the edge, soaring into a peak of pleasure.

My eyes were wet when I opened them, my body still shaking from the burst of euphoria. Zekiel stood still as a statue, one hand on my inner thigh. “Will you have dinner with me tonight?”

Those words were unexpected, considering what had just happened. “Yes,” I whispered.

Helping me sit up, he covered me with the cloak. “Good.” He lifted my hand and brushed his lips over my knuckles. “Until tonight.”

20

CELESTE

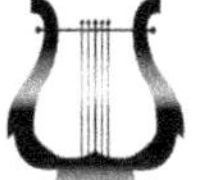

In a dreamlike state, I walked the garden paths back to the castle, my mind reeling with what had just happened. I waited for a pang of guilt or regret, but I only felt a sense of giddiness, fully aware that I wanted more.

Petra was waiting for me on the balcony, and I realized it was only the second time I'd seen the gnome. She gave me a relieved smile as I approached. "There you are," she breathed. "I was worried. Zekiel asked me to check on you, but I got held up in the kitchens."

"Petra," I said, climbing the stairs toward her, my face warm as my tongue stumbled over the next words. "I've just come from speaking with Zekiel. He invited me to dine with him tonight."

Petra clasped her hands together and beamed. "Oh, that's a fine thing. I will help you prepare."

I held open the cloak, showing her my ripped dress.

"I could use some help. The vines attacked me and ruined this gown."

Petra made a face. "Nasty plants. I'm sorry to hear that, but I know what will make it better. Come with me to the kitchens. Hinko just made cinnamon buns. I'll bribe him for a few, and we'll have tea."

My spirits brightened at the idea of doing something civil. "I'd like that."

Despite her being only three feet tall, I felt much safer with Petra as we navigated the passageways of the castle to the kitchen. The scent of cinnamon accosted us before we arrived, and we swept into a bright room, sunlight beaming down on long tables that could seat at least twenty. Elaborate chandeliers hung from the ceiling, gems glittering like stars in the night sky.

Adjoining doors opened to a kitchen, and just through the doorway was Hinko, a dark-headed gnome, spreading icing across buns. I remembered seeing him the night I'd first arrived and having the distinct sense he was rather surly and unfriendly.

"Have a seat." Petra waved at the table. "I'll be right back with a tray."

She disappeared into the kitchen while I sank into a velvet chair, examining the radiance around me. The hall was meant to host the entire court, yet it struck me again that I was alone.

I listened, but no growls came, and with the sun shining into the room, it was hard to believe anything bad happened in the castle.

A memory of my father's palace burst into my mind, and I pressed my hand against my head. I hadn't believed anything bad could happen there either, but then Vivian came along, tall and slender and beautiful. Her presence was like the sun, warming everything that surrounded her, but if one stayed too long, they eventually got burned, or, in my father's case, poisoned. I'd always wondered what drove her, whether it was a desire to rule or madness.

"You look thoughtful." Petra's voice broke into my thoughts as she put a tray on the table. "Here, have a tea."

She set a steaming cup down in front of me and then settled into a chair across from me, using a pillow to prop herself up.

Wrapping my fingers around the warmth of the mug, I studied her, wondering if I might have an ally. Fairies were treacherous, Yosa was full of words but shared very little information about Irradiance, and Petra, well, I didn't know her at all. Conversation had always been my weakness. I didn't know where to start, aside from bumbling into a blunt question. "What do you do here?"

Petra relaxed against the back of a chair, as though she were used to having tea with strangers. "Oh, I keep the castle clean, and Hinko cooks."

"You keep the entire castle clean by yourself?"

Petra giggled. "Bless you, it's not as hard as you think."

"I admit, I haven't explored every nook and cranny, but it seems immense."

"It is, but Hinko and I only work up here in the main areas. We rarely venture down to Irradiance, but you've been there. What did you think?"

"It's lovely, but I missed the sunshine."

"I agree; the gems are bewitching but nothing can replace daylight."

"How long have you worked here? Or for Zekiel?"

Petra shrugged. "It's been a long time. Usually, when refugees come to the castle, Zekiel finds a place for them within a week or two, but I was drawn to this place. I wanted to stay and he allowed me to."

I leaned forward. "Refugees? From where? Was there a war that drove them here?"

"Bless you," Petra said around a mouthful of a cinnamon bun. "No, it's just his job, you know? Irradiance is a sanctuary kingdom for those fleeing their former lives. Some run from war, others from abuse and persecution, to escape death or start a new life. Whatever it may be, they come here."

It suddenly dawned on me that I could be counted as a refugee. "Is that why it's so empty here, because they've all gone to their new homes?"

"It's not always quiet like this," Petra said, sorrow passing over her bright face. "There used to be others here once, but now. . ."

"It's too dangerous?" I filled in.

Her eyes widened. "Did he tell you?"

I nodded, trying to loosen her tongue by making her think I knew more than I did. "I'm here to help."

A funny expression crossed her face, as though she wanted to wrinkle her nose against a bad smell but refrained. "I was surprised you went wandering the garden paths without an escort."

"I learned my lesson, but the fairies didn't warn me."

Petra snorted. "Is this your first encounter with fairies?"

"In this land, yes."

Leaning forward, Petra lowered her voice. "Fairies used to be loyal, but now they are more mischievous than ever. They'll play tricks on you for no reason other than their own amusement, and they are always listening. Be careful what you say and what promises you make to them. The thinking is that perhaps their allegiance lies elsewhere, and they stay here as spies."

"Why?" I whispered back. "What enemies does Zekiel have?"

Petra shrugged and answered in her normal speaking voice. "A king will always have enemies. Jealousy, corruption, the desire to gain lands and wealth, it all breeds controversy, especially in a land like this. I'm sure whoever you were running from would be delighted if they could catch you here, but they can't."

I recalled Zekiel's words about being safe from my former life. I had no idea he had such a noble position of power, to protect and rescue others from their circumstances. All this while, I'd assumed he'd stolen me for some wicked purpose, but now, I realized he was saving me from the forest.

"Does he always make a contract with everyone who comes here?"

"Well of course. It's a way of proving oneself."

"So then where are we, in relation to the natural world?"

Petra giggled. "You and I come from quite different worlds, so if I explained where Irradiance sits compared to the mountain of gnomes, it would make no sense to you."

I bit into a cinnamon bun and the richness of sugar and butter melted in my mouth. Suddenly, I didn't want to be bothered by my troubles anymore.

"Will you tell me about the mountain of gnomes and where you came from?"

Petra settled back in her chair and told me stories of her people, and as she spoke, she didn't seem like a servant at all, but someone who had willingly chosen to stay in Irradiance. Just like Yosa, and, I supposed, Ryder, and the many gnomes who worked the mine, which meant that Zekiel wasn't some kind of monster, but a savior set on some dark quest.

Staring into my cup of tea, I recalled his lips on mine, the urgency there, the need. My pulse quickened in anticipation of being in his presence again.

21

CELESTE

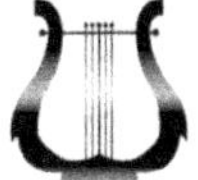

Petra stayed with me through the rest of the day and helped me dress for dinner. A wardrobe within my room revealed rows and rows of dresses. Petra picked out a grown made of silver and gold thread. She braided my hair into a crown on top of my head, leaving a few curls hanging loose. When I looked in the mirror, I felt not just like royalty but beautiful. Even the length of my hair didn't bother me anymore, and the hollowness was gone from my eyes.

Being in Zekiel's land was changing me, and I took a deep breath, wondering if he would kiss me again, and whether our sensual exploration would go much further tonight.

Petra left me, not in the dining hall, but in the smaller, more intimate room where I'd signed the contract. Night had fallen, but the shadows were chased away by soft candles hanging from the ceiling and lighting up one end of the table where two places were set: Zekiel, I imagined at the head, and myself at his right side.

Aside from myself, the room was empty, but the door to the balcony was ajar. The mellow tones of harp music drifted to my ears with an intoxicating pull. My entire body relaxed, and my heart leaped with yearning. Before I knew it, I'd taken a few steps toward the melody, as though it were something physical I could reach out and grab hold of.

I swayed to the rhythm, watching the flames leap and dance as though they, too, swayed to the same melodies. A breeze blew and a few of the candles closest to the balcony went out. It was then I noticed my host sat on the balustrade, gazing into the darkness as he played.

His hair shone in the moonlight, and he wore a royal blue shirt, the edges trimmed with gold. I swallowed hard, watching him play. The beauty of the music and the sorrow with which he played made my heart ache. Unlike the night I'd met him, he didn't appear like some horned monster, full of tricks, but a man of flesh and blood, with a broken heart.

All this time, my focus had been on my needs, and I hadn't considered his tale. Had he always been destined to be king over this strange kingdom? I was certain he had a heart, and I wanted to unlock the deep well of emotion he kept guarded. The more I learned about him, the more I yearned for a deeper understanding.

I wiped the moisture from my eyes and backed away like an intruder. He'd invited me to dine with him, but I couldn't shake the sense that something was terribly wrong. Did an evil lurk here, intent on destroying Zekiel's kingdom? If I asked him directly, would he share the truth with me?

A niggling within told me that my thought was arrogant, as if I, a lowly princess of nothing, could gain the trust of a king whom the gnomes and fairies obeyed. What we shared in the greenhouse did not entitle me to his confidence.

A light step drew my attention back to the patio. Zekiel stepped inside, carrying a harp in his hands. This one wasn't the smaller lyre he'd taken through the portal, but a larger harp he carried with both hands. He shut the door behind him, and when he faced me, his smokey gray eyes were misty, like mountains before the sunrise burned away the fog.

"Celeste," he said, voice hoarse. "I'm pleased to see you."

A thrill of hope shot through my veins and my voice died in my throat. *Pleased*. To see *me*?

He set the harp to the side and pulled out my chair for me. "I hope I didn't keep you waiting long."

"No, not at all," I answered rather breathlessly, stepping closer to him. "I enjoyed the music."

His gray eyes were still dark, but the sharp lines

around his mouth softened, then flitted up in a ghost of a smile. A sudden reminder of his fingers against my skin made desire coil deep within. Were we going to talk about what happened in the greenhouse?

Zekiel took a seat at the head of the table. "Do you play?"

No. Then maybe later. I leaned against the back of the chair in an attempt to relax. "Not anymore. I've always been fond of music, but my father said it was a waste of time, for me at least. During dinners or balls, I was to be part of the action, not stand or sit in a corner playing music."

"You may play here if it pleases you."

"That is very generous, but I'd never be able to play as effortlessly as you do."

"You doubt your talent, yet we all begin somewhere. Music has been a particular passion of mine, but it was only consistent practice that led me to become a master of the harp."

I struggled to figure out how to tell him it wasn't the practice that found me lacking, but before I formed a response, Hinko and Petra appeared with the first course. It was a light, verdant soup with a sprinkling of crispy onions on top and sweet wine to go with it. Petra winked at me as she sat down a tray, and together, the two gnomes left us in peace.

We ate in measured silence for a few moments, enough time to make nerves flutter in my stomach again. "Will you teach me?" I asked softly.

Zekiel froze, studying me. "Teach you? To play the harp?"

"Yes," I nodded.

A slow smile softened his marble-like features. "That is not the sort of payment request I expected from you."

"Well, since the treasury is off limits..." I quipped, trying to lighten the mood.

Instead of replying, his gaze shifted to the closed doors of the balcony. I'd said something wrong, but instead of closing my mouth, I blundered on. "Did you expect me to ask for a bag of gems? I supposed it would be wiser to take them with me when this is all over."

"I give all who complete their contracts a bag of gems."

"Ah, so all who come here are given a contract. Then why are you called the King of Hearts?"

Zekiel paused as the second course was served, a green salad with fresh tomatoes drizzled with a sweet basil sauce. Once Hinko and Petra had left, he spoke again. "You are quite curious about me, aren't you? You don't mince words."

"You're unlike any king I've ever met."

"Oh, and you've met many kings?"

I made a face. "Well, no. My presence at court embarrassed my father, and he did not allow me to travel."

Zekiel's eyes narrowed. "Why was he embarrassed

by you?"

My stomach soured. I clenched my hands in my lap, remembering. "I'm…odd. Things happened when I was at court, during dinners."

"Things like what?"

I paused, considering how truthful to be. "My father complained I was too blunt and straightforward to carry a conversation in court, but it was important I was present. Instead of conversing, I began to play music, but strange things happened. Once, the china floated off a tray. Another time, all the windows in the room shattered, and a third time, a flock of birds murdered themselves on a castle wall. Father forbade me from touching a string."

Zekiel paused, fork frozen in the air as he listened, giving me his full attention. "Curious," he whispered, half to himself, half to me.

"I never intended to be a nuisance, but sitting in dull political meetings wasn't particularly enjoyable," I finished hastily, uncomfortable with how deeply he stared into me.

"What did you enjoy?"

"Riding horses, playing music. I always longed to travel."

"All those things you can accomplish here."

The lightness in his tone made me look at him. "True. Not exactly in the way I intended, though. Will you tell me what haunts your kingdom?"

Finishing his salad, he leaned back and swirled the

wine in the glass. "You are a princess. Surely you know that secrets are told to only a few close advisors, no one else. I understand your curiosity; you've been asked to steal precious relics, and you wonder why."

"Yes." I picked up my full glass of wine. Originally, I'd decided not to drink, but now, I wanted something to help me keep my courage. Bubbles rose to the top and a peachy scent wafted to my nose. I took a sip, letting it bloom on my tongue. "You're a bit of an oxymoron. You take in refugees and give them a new home, yet I'm your thief."

"Ah, you've discovered one of my secrets. The work you do helps keep this realm safe."

"I might have guessed as much. You've very vague and protective, but why? What troubles your realm that you are forced to steal like a criminal?"

He leaned closer, and I caught a whiff of mint and something oaky. Wood. I tilted my chin up, prepared for a fight, but there was that softness in his smokey eyes. No, not a softness: sadness. It threw me off guard.

"Tell me, Celeste," he purred. "Why were you running through the shadow wood? I felt your need for me, your desire to escape from whatever haunted you. You must have been very desperate indeed to risk your life like that."

Stunned, I sat down the wineglass. I'd assumed that because he knew my name, he knew about my past, but that wasn't true. He wanted to hear my story from my lips and then, he might share his with me. It was a signal of trust.

"I..." I began, but Hinko and Petra burst in with the main course.

It was an entire roasted duck with a citrus sauce and tiny potatoes surrounding it. Hinko sat it down in front of Zekiel, who took up a knife to carve it. "Thank you. If you leave the wine, that will be all," he said.

I might have imagined it, but I thought the lights burned lower as Zekiel slid a slice of duck onto my plate, along with a generous helping of the sauce and potatoes. A restless energy burned within me as I stared at the food, and suddenly, I wanted to tell him.

"I used to be afraid to eat a meal like this," I explained. "I was worried I'd be poisoned and die. I suppose I suspected my father's new wife from the start, but I tried to tell myself it was only jealousy. My mother died long ago. I barely remember her, except that she always smelled of flowers. Father kept her gardens for a long time, and he held off remarrying, although I overheard him arguing with his advisors about how he needed sons."

"Ah, sons. It is both a blessing and a curse for human royalty."

I took another sip of wine. "In my case, it was a curse. Eventually, a woman named Vivian appeared from another kingdom. I don't recall if she had a title before. In fact, under her presence, the entire court was bewitched. Vivian was so beautiful, everyone else paled in comparison, and she captured my father's attention. He'd always loved me in his own way, but after Vivian came, we barely spoke two words. They were quickly married, and she took over more of his duties as he grew sick and weak. It was a terrible death, and I wasn't allowed to visit, but I heard his cries and moans. When it was over, Vivian became Queen. She was crowned fast, because she suspected foul play. I was locked in my chamber and forgotten, except the Queen still visited. Looking back, I think I knew what was happening all along, but the truth was too horrible to consider. Now, I realize her visits were so she could gain the courage to harm me. It was a huntress who set me free. She appeared in the dead of night and told me the Queen was jealous of my beauty and wanted to eat my heart. It sounded like a tale out of a storybook, but I believed every word. So, I ran. I only entered the shadow wood to throw the hunters off my scent. Then, you appeared."

He'd been quiet through my story, and now I dared a glance at him, surprised to see the sorrow flickering in the depths of his gaze. "You were desperate enough to put your life in danger to save yourself. I'm only doing the same thing with my kingdom."

I swallowed hard and my chest went tight. I'd laid myself bare and that was his only response.

However, Zekiel wasn't finished. His fingertips grazed my wrist in an act of unspoken sympathy, his very touch awakening my senses, making me burn for him again.

"Hear me now, Celeste," he said. "The burdens of my kingdom are heavy, and I would not share that load with you. What you went through, losing your father and your kingdom, is more than any should have to bear. I would not add to your grief. Do not ask, because I will not change my mind. Know this: you were brave, and you did the right thing. I'm honored you're here in my kingdom, and I'm honored to have dinner with you. Your presence is comforting and never an embarrassment."

I blinked hard, biting my lip at the words he spoke. I caught his fingers with mine and squeezed his hand, hoping he understood what those words meant to me. "Thank you."

22

CELESTE

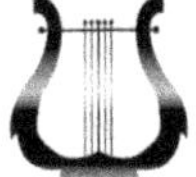

My appetite returned and we continued dinner, speaking only of light affairs. Zekiel told me about his lands and gardens, including the greenhouse with herbs and vegetables, the vineyard he tended to, and the brilliant flower gardens that carpeted the ground right up to the lush forest.

The longer we sat and talked, the more relaxed and at ease I felt. Zekiel was easy to talk to, and conversation flowed between us. At last came the moment. Zekiel stood and held out a hand to me. "May I escort you to your room?"

"You may," I said, placing my hand on his arm.

I imagined us returning to my room, where I'd invite him into my chamber. It was inappropriate and scandalous, but not something I had to worry about since I was no longer in the land of mortals. I couldn't quite pinpoint my intense attraction to him, aside from the fact that he was the first man who had given me undivided attention.

As a princess, I expected to have many suitors, princes from other kingdoms, counts and dukes to flirt with me at balls. Instead, I'd been ignored, hidden away, and the only person who gave me attention was Queen Vivian, apparently jealous that I was more beautiful than she. But what was beauty if no one saw it or praised it?

Here, no one had remarked on my appearance, and from the conversation with Zekiel, even he looked beyond the surface, as though interested in my soul. It left me feeling somewhat ashamed I'd judged him so quickly when he sprung out of the ground and stole me away. I'd have to stop using the word *stolen*, because he'd really saved me.

All too soon, we arrived outside the door of my borrowed chamber. Zekiel slid his gloved hand down my back, sending shivers up my spine as he pressed me closer to him. My breath stole away as I lifted my face to his, thinking how handsome he looked in the low light, his gaze deep with hidden emotion, his hand pressing me firmly against him. A tingling began in my belly, and a sweet ache grew. Would he take me fully tonight?

"I enjoyed dinner with you, Celeste," he murmured, tucking a loose curl behind my ear.

"And I with you," I whispered, captivated by his presence.

The warmth of his palm touched my cheek, and his thumb brushed my lips, almost making me moan aloud. A delicious tension passed between us, and yet we remained frozen in indecision. Only one move, one heartbeat away from taking the next step. Would he make the next move, or should I be so bold?

Here, in a land where I had nothing to lose, why not?

I rose on my tiptoes like a dancer and pressed my lips firmly against his.

Zekiel let out a sigh and kissed me back with an intensity that left me breathless. He backed me against the wall, claiming me with his mouth, his hands on my back moving lower to grip my bottom, pressing his hardness into me.

I moaned into his mouth as our tongues twisted in an intoxicating dance. He tasted like sweet wine, and the strength of his arms made me feel as though nothing could harm me. My body sang like taut harp strings under his touch, and I ached to belong to him fully.

Lacing my fingers around his neck, I held on, pressing my chest against his, ready to invite him inside.

Shadows flickered around us, and then came a menacing growl.

Zekiel broke the kiss, his entire body rigid as he clasped me tightly in his arms. My head rested against his heart, and I felt the uptick of his pulse as he took a shuddering breath. The absence of his lips left me bereft, but he was so solid, so real. There it came again, that same guttural growl I'd heard earlier.

Zekiel cursed and then released me.

A hardness had returned to his features as he stepped back, giving me a half bow. "Duty calls. Sleep well, Celeste; we leave for the next task tomorrow afternoon."

Then, he was gone, slipping through the shadows while I leaned against the door, panting as his moonlight hair faded away. I pushed away deep disappointment, determined not to cry. He hadn't told me no, but he had chosen his work over me. That growl might have belonged to a demented creature in the castle, but if I asked about it, Zekiel would once again refuse to share.

With a heavy sigh, I slipped inside, locking the door behind me. In the room, a cozy fire burned, and the gauzy nightgown the fairies had woven lay on the bed. I shrugged out of the dress and made my way to the washbasin just as the sound of bells came.

Hada skipped across the water, flinging droplets at me before she perched on the looking glass.

"I spied you having dinner with the king," she announced, crossing her arms. "If I didn't think any better, and if we hadn't made a deal to help each other, I'd think you were rather enamored by him."

Had she spied us kissing? I bit my tongue to keep my retort inside, fingers shaking as I unbraided my hair

—I'd forgotten all about the deal. "I have to be amicable. You and I both know my contract is with him, and a breach of contract brings undesirable consequences."

"Yet that's exactly what you asked for: a way to escape, is it not? Or have you fallen in love?"

"Hardly," I protested. "I'm new to this realm, and these kinds of things take time. If you'd rather not work together, we can be done."

"Oh, but we can't. Fairies don't go back on their words."

I swallowed hard, recalling Petra's words. "What would happen if I changed my mind?"

Hada snorted. "If you change your mind, you'll be sorry. Very, very sorry. Don't you know that I have the power to make your life miserable?"

I bristled. "Like when you failed to warn me about the vines in the greenhouse, and how they'd attack me?"

"Ah, you're a prickly princess. Strangers don't fare well here." Hada rose and flitted across the room. "Don't forget my warning to you. Keep the deal and you'll live in peace. Break it, and, well, I'll have a word or two with the king about how two-faced you are."

She disappeared before I could say anything else, but anger flared up, burning away the buzz of pleasant feelings from the heated kisses Zekiel and I had shared. Half-dressed, I paced, weighing my options.

I'd been rash in trusting a fairy. I should come clean and tell Zekiel the truth, but what would he do with me? I didn't think I could bear the weight of his disappointment.

I settled into bed with one thought: I needed to speak to Yosa. She'd give me clear advice and spending some time in Irradiance would give me a reprieve from the fairies. Except I wouldn't be able to see Zekiel. I touched two fingers to my lips and fell back into the pillows with a groan.

23

CELESTE

I dreamed of Zekiel, with his long hair shining like the moonlight. When I threaded my fingers through the silky strands, it glimmered like a pearl, as though he were the king of jewels. He pressed his hand against my back, that same gentleness in his face and dark sorrow haunting his gray eyes. Bending his horned head near mine, he claimed my lips, and all my anxiety melted away into passion. I moved, clinging to him, my entire body on fire with a burning need.

The dream shifted and suddenly, I lay on my back while he rose above me, only my thin nightgown between us. My legs clenched around him, drawing him closer, desperate, needing. He paused, head hovering above mine, studying me with an intensity, as though he were deciding. When he brushed his gloved hand down my cheek, my fingers closed around his and I drew the glove off.

White bone rose before me, and then he turned into a skeleton, a grinning skull with horns and eyeless sockets leaning closer to take me, claim me. A scream of horror rose from my chest, and I bucked, trying to push him off me, but boney fingers closed around my wrists, and a deep, layered voice growled, "Submit."

I woke covered in sweat, hands clawing at my throat for air. Stumbling out of bed, I went to the window and threw open the curtains, letting in the pale glow of dawn. After that nightmare, I couldn't be in the dark a moment more. Pouring a glass of water, I took a shaky drink before lying back down, my face to the window. I lay until the shaking subsided and the haze of fear receded.

It was only a dream, but it had felt so real.

I hadn't considered what had happened to Zekiel's arm, and I shuddered to think he might have a withered hand underneath his glove.

A sound at the door drew my attention, a soft scratching noise. Heart in my throat, I slid out of bed and dressed. I wouldn't let my fears overtake me, not this time. I opened the door into the empty hall, seeing a spot of white laying at my feet. A scroll. I picked it up and out fell a golden necklace with a pendant of a harp.

Zekiel?

I held it in my palm, and tiny gems glittered in the morning light. It was a tiny replica of a golden harp, with delicate swirls along the edges, while the background was a midnight sky, diamonds twinkling like stars. I slipped the necklace over my head, feeling the cool jewel between my breasts, and unrolled the scroll. The handwriting must be his, elegant calligraphy with his name scribbled at the bottom.

Celeste - as a token of gratitude, here is a gift for you. I hope you'll wear it often and always. Here's the route to my hall of harps. Enjoy. – Zekiel.

The scent of leather and ink drifted from the scroll, and I rolled it back up, my heart pounding. He'd written it as though it were a letter to a lover, and the gift! My heart leaped in my chest as I clutched the necklace. It was only a confirmation that he returned my budding feelings, and the token meant the contract was more than a cold business transaction.

Holding up the note, I studied the directions to his hall of harps and my stomach fluttered. There were no signs of the malicious presence from yesterday, nor of those damned fairies. Breakfast could wait. I slipped into the hall and followed Zekiel's instructions.

Walls shimmered with light, guiding my way, but the castle reminded silent, a hollowed vessel, bleak and empty of inhabitants. It left me feeling sad that Zekiel had few people to share his wealth with, at least not up here. Still, the longer I walked, the more a sense of unease grew, as though something was watching.

At last, I reached double doors. For a moment, I feared I'd lost my way, but a glimmer came as the doors opened, steadily growing brighter until I made out the shape of a dizzying array of harps. There were small ones, tiny enough to hold, and larger ones to sit at. Some of them were plain, others gilded gold with designs carved into them. There weren't just one or two but dozens of them, filling the cavern. This truly was a hall of harps.

Leaving the doors open, I walked along the instruments, trailing my fingers over the smooth wood, plucking a note here and there, a melody creeping out of the darkness. With each note, the room grew brighter, as though the vibrations of the notes provided light.

Apprehension filled me and I hesitated to play, until I reminded myself I wasn't in my father's kingdom anymore. What had happened there might not happen here. Taking a deep breath, I sat down at one of the larger ones, wondering if my fingers would recall the notes.

The scent of wood filled my nose, and I took a deep breath, inhaling. A sense of peace filled me as my fingers stroked the strings, and memories long buried returned. I wasn't as skillful as Zekiel, and my progress was slow as I searched for the correct notes. As the halting melody filled the hall, my anxiety faded.

Closing my eyes, I focused on the melody, a memory of my father shouting and ladies wailing coming to mind. I recalled the shattered glass, dripping blood, and the way others began to treat me differently. My fingers slipped off the strings as I thought of how the small act of playing music had alienated me. I didn't have any genuine friendships with the courtesans. They—like the fairies—rang of falsehood, kind to my face while gossiping about my oddities behind my back. My stomach soured with the reminder that a gift was never simply a gift. The ones in the palace came with a price, a favor, a dance, a stolen kiss, and sometimes, a future promise.

Tears burned the back of my eyes, but I refused to let them fall. Time was wasted feeling sorry for myself, especially when I was determined to define my own future. I hoped that perhaps my oddities would allow me to blend into this magical world.

When I looked up from the harp, Zekiel stood in the doorway, dressed in an open plum shirt. The deep v of the cut showed off his bare chest, and a tingle of irritation rose as I stood, wondering how long he'd been standing there, watching, listening.

Anger punctured my words as I held up the necklace. "Is this a gift? Or another way for you to entrap me?"

A shadow crossed his angular face, and his eyes went hard. "It's a gift, nothing more. If you don't like it..."

I'd insulted him. Horror and embarrassment swept through me. I'd forgotten how close we were last night and allowed the foul memories of the past to shape my response. "I'm sorry. It's just, where I come from, acceptance of a gift means you owe the giver something."

Zekiel crossed his arms. "You owe me nothing."

I stared down at the harp, ears burning. "I…I love it, truly I do. It was thoughtful of you, and to share this with me." I waved my hands to indicate the room.

"I listened to you play; you have talent."

I dared to glance at him and although his expression was still unreadable, he'd stepped into the room.

"My skills are rudimentary compared to yours."

"Nothing that can't be fixed with practice. You are welcome to come here as often as you like."

"Thank you. Where did you collect these from? I've never seen so many harps in one place."

This time his features softened. "I made them."

My jaw dropped. "You're not the kind of king I expected."

"I imagine not. I'm nothing like the mortals." He grinned, displaying a flash of his fangs.

He'd kissed me with those wicked sharp teeth and if only my response had been warmer and more welcoming, he might do so again. Why did I have to be odd and awkward? "How do you find time to make harps?" I asked. "You're a king. I don't pretend to know what you do with your time, but you must be busy.

Shouldn't this be the kind of hard work you delegate to someone else?"

"I've heard that mortal kings and queens sit above their subjects, selecting the best from the land, growing rich on the back-breaking work of their citizens. They grow soft, focused on festivities, wars, and political banter, bargains to increase their land and wealth and titles. They don't take time to know the land, work it, or get their hands dirty. In this realm, everyone works, for how is one to know how to lead people if they do not understand their joys and struggles, or what their work is like? For myself, I find it important to work with my hands. Once, I wasn't a king; I was merely a worker, and I don't forget those times."

"Where I come from, no one has that perspective."

"There is also magic here. You accused me of offering the necklace as more than a gift, and you're right: it's a token of protection."

My fingers closed around it. "Protection from what?"

"As you suspected, there is evil that lurks both inside and outside my realm. Since we leave tonight, it is my duty to protect you."

My heart kicked and the words were out of my mouth before I could stop them. "Is it your duty or something else?"

He took a step back, studying me. When at last he spoke, his voice was low. "I did not expect to like you, so yes, it is my duty, and...more."

I sucked in a deep breath, undone by his words.

"For now, I take my leave of you. Stay inside today. It's safer. Petra will help you prepare, and I'll find you. Soon."

He bowed his head and moved in a whisper of a breath. I watched his pale hair drift behind me as I touched another finger to the string of the harp.

24

ZEKIEL

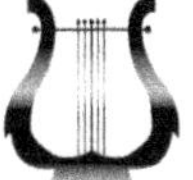

Something strange had happened. She played the harp, and it called me to her. One moment, I'd been in my study, the next, I was involuntarily walking, lured to my room of harps as though she'd called my name.

It rang out like a bell, and there she was, playing the biggest harp. Not well, but not terribly either, struggling with the melody. As I told her, practice and a bit of instruction would help her become better. I was still trying to puzzle out why her playing summoned me.

I quickened my steps, ears acute to the tune of the harp, but no more sounds rang out, and it left me with nothing but curiosity.

Perhaps I should have stayed or given her a small lesson, or attempted to prepare her for tonight myself. Instead, a nagging thought warned me about getting too close to the princess. I wasn't supposed to like her or care for her in any way, yet I found myself falling. She was supposed to be a means to an end, nothing more. Here for a year and then gone, elsewhere, on to a better life.

During dinner last night, it had been too easy to open up to her. She shared the woes of her past and I, in turn, told her about my realm and how proud I was of what I'd built. A beautiful haven, a place where all came to rest, restart, and set off, emboldened with confidence to achieve their purpose in life.

Decades of hard work would be in vain when the sorceress' curse was complete. I'd be trapped, no longer able to come and go as I pleased. Eventually, death would swallow my realm in its withering grasp, and everyone would be forced to flee. When I succeeded, those who I'd sent away could return.

In order to win, I had to risk *her* life. No one would miss Princess Celeste, for she was as good as dead. The tasks I asked of her were dangerous, with a low possibility of her coming out unscathed in the end. I was supposed to use her for my purposes, but instead, I'd kissed her, and now I cared. Guilt crept around me; the plan was set in motion, and it was too late to change or divert the course. I was king and people counted on me to save them, but what if I couldn't save the one person who finally mattered more to me than anything?

25

CELESTE

Petra brought me new clothes for the second task, yet another pair of leathers, but this time with pants instead of a skirt and boots that went up to my calves. I felt almost boyish dressed in such a way, and I wondered what sort of situation I'd be in this time. So far, nothing had come of the stolen relic and the so-called curse of Viridis. I assumed it was due to being in a magical realm and the portals that kept the monks from finding us. Still, a beat of dread went through me at what I'd have to steal next.

The journey to Irradiance was faster this time, although the staircase to the sacred gates still left me breathless. When the specter appeared, I turned away, but the sound of her slurping Zekiel's blood was loud in the hushed silence. Mouth stained crimson, she called out the arcane spell and the gates appeared.

Zekiel took my arm and led me to the second

entrance, where we passed into a starlit night. I lifted my face to milk-white moonlight as a faint breeze stirred, sending the scent of sweet honeysuckle to my nose.

"Do you know where we are?" Zekiel asked, fingers grazing the small of my back.

I glanced around the spare wood, the dark shapes of trees leading up a hill, and then realized what I'd assumed was moonlight was something else entirely. We stood at the base of a domed hill, and at the very top glowed a white light. My stomach dipped as I raked my mind for memory of a place with a replica of the moon.

"No, but you've been here before?"

"I have," Zekiel said.

"Do we have twenty-four hours to return again? The Mistress of the Portal didn't mention it."

"We do. That is always the time limit when one goes through the sacred portals."

I studied him, standing so close, it made my heart ache. The light reflected off his hair, but the shadows hid his face. "That wasn't always the case, was it?"

"No, the time limit is solely for me. That is why Ryder goes comes and goes as he pleases. Speaking of, he should join us shortly with further instructions."

"Ah," I said, recalling the explosion outside the temple. Ryder, of course, was responsible. "Will you tell me what you want me to retrieve for you this time?"

"It's not that you should be afraid." He shifted closer to me until our arms touched.

I swallowed hard. "I can't help but be nervous. Are you going to spell this place with your harp?"

"No. A heist cannot be done in the same way twice. It is likely that a few have guessed what is happening and are prepared. They will ensure each relic is closely guarded, and those who surrounded it will ward themselves against magic."

"That doesn't make me feel any better," I muttered.

"Then you should know tonight is a celebratory night in this region. Midnight marks the first day of spring."

Spring. Had winter fled so fast?

"There will be feasting and celebrations," Zekiel went on. "Of course, precautions have been taken to protect the relic, but how ironic that a symbol of luck will be taken on the very night they celebrate it. Do you hear it?"

Faintly came the thud of drums, and I suddenly felt ill at the idea of interrupting a celebration and stealing the stone that gave them hope. "It's a moonstone, isn't it? You want me to steal it."

Zekiel nodded. "The light you see isn't the moon, but the stone. They've used mirrors to magnify it, make it appear brighter this night."

"They'll know when it's gone," I protested.

"True. The Solaris Luna is unique, but its light can be replicated with a gem." He pressed a bag into my hands. "You'll need to make the swap as soon as the opportunity presents itself."

Of course, Zekiel was prepared for this exact moment. I scowled, not exactly at him, but at the situation I found myself in. Escape seemed a better alternative than stealing from helpless mortals. Perhaps I needed to redouble my efforts to find the treasury and the rosebud jewel for Hada. Damn my attraction to Zekiel. Was it worth it for this sin? Surely there would be another man who made my blood sing.

"Zekiel. Celeste." A rough male voice interrupted, and a shadow moved toward us.

Zekiel stepped away from me. "Ryder."

"There's a bit of an issue," Ryder announced, stopping a few paces away.

I folded in on myself. If there was a problem, perhaps Zekiel would call off the heist and we could return to Irradiance.

"What's happened?" Zekiel asked.

"It's the location of the relic. They used to keep it in the dome. That's what we planned for, but they've moved it to a tower, heavily guarded."

"How many?"

"On the outside, ten guards and five hounds. On the inside, I can only guess how many, but it doesn't matter. There's a narrow staircase that leads to the top, meaning any fight would have to be one on one, and going up would be brutal."

Zekiel folded his arms. "Is the tower on sacred land too?"

"It is, unfortunately, or I would not hesitate. You and I could easily overwhelm the guards."

"We need a new plan then, and quickly."

"I've considered an airborne assault, but we didn't bring the beasts."

"No, and regardless, they would end up in trouble."

Ryder dropped his voice. "There is another option."

Zekiel stepped closer to him; voices low, they discussed while I stood back, holding the bag and waiting. I glanced at the wood, wondering if I should bolt. I still didn't know where I was, and the shadows felt creepy. Alternatively, there was the celebration taking place in the dome. I could become one of them, lost in the rites. If I were in a sacred place, Zekiel could do nothing. I couldn't shake the sense that this theft was wrong, yet running from Zekiel felt like a betrayal.

They finished speaking, and Ryder bounded off into the night while Zekiel returned to my side. My chin trembled and I couldn't look at him.

"This will not be as straightforward as last time," he apologized.

"Why not wait?"

"Wait for what? Another day? Another opportunity? There is none. Every day we don't act increases the opportunity that someone else might come to steal this relic."

"It's dangerous."

"I am aware, but I will keep you as safe as I possibly can."

"You can't promise that, especially when I go into a sacred place you cannot enter."

"Which is why you won't be entering the tower. It's too great of a risk."

His words stunned me, and I faced him as he sat down on a fallen log. I joined him. "There's one thing I don't understand: why me?"

Zekiel took my hand and held it between his bare hand and his gloved one. "Do you doubt your importance in this world? If only you knew how important you are."

Maybe it was his touch or perhaps it was his words, but my heart glowed. Suddenly, I wanted to try. No one ever needed or wanted me, but the way he drew me toward him made my heart skip a beat. "I didn't think you'd care what happened to your thief, as long as you got your relics."

"I care," he said. "So very much."

26

CELESTE

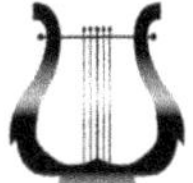

We waited in the wood for a while until a hawk flew down and Zekiel rose. "It's time."

I followed him down an invisible path, my heart still ringing with those two little words: *I care.* My heart was conflicted, torn between two choices. Knowing he cared only increased my desire to stay, yet awareness of what was to come made me want to flee. I wasn't a thief, nor did I belong in an immortal realm. When the opportunity arose, I needed to seize it and flee, but no one had ever taken the time to see me the way he did, and it was intoxicating.

The beat of the drums continued, ebbing and flowing in various rhythms, but light bloomed bright as we came to a tower. It was perched on a hill, no trees around it, the open space displaying the guards marching back and forth, joined by hounds with glowing eyes.

I went cold all over. Zekiel would not make me go in there, not with the guards. What was his plan?

His fingers closed around my wrist as he drew me closer to his solid bulk. "When it happens, you have to run. Find the stone, swap it with the jewel, and return to me. I'll draw out the guards and keep them from attacking you."

"When what happens?" I begged.

Instead of answering, he placed his hands on my shoulders. Together, we walked to the very edge of the clearing, facing the tower. On the ground lay a bow and arrow, which Zekiel picked up as though it were a gift left purposefully for him. He effortlessly notched an arrow in his bow and moved to my side.

"You can do this," he said. "I know it's different from before, but I believe in you."

A roaring boom smote the air. Throwing my hand over my head, I screamed and tried to duck, but suddenly, Zekiel's arm was around my waist. He held me tightly against his chest as a thunderous sound shook the area. Tree trunks swayed, and a rattle of dead leaves cascaded around us. The light from the moonstone flicked out, followed by sharp barks and shouts.

Every bone in my body trembled, but Zekiel's voice was a command in my ear. "Run."

Swallowing down my fear, I forced eyes open. Where the tower had once stood was a mere pile of rock and rubble. Somehow, someway, Ryder must have created an explosion that took down the tower, a feat which should have been impossible, but I was beginning to understand the wildness of magic. Amidst the rubble, I spied a faint glow. The relic.

"It's now or never," Zekiel urged me.

It was only then that he let go of me. Borrowing his strength and knowing what was expected of me, I made my legs move. I bolted out of the wood like a hunted rabbit, and seconds later, I heard the whoosh of an arrow speed past me.

Run. Don't think. Just act.

One glaring question stubbornly forced its way to the forefront of my mind, a question I'd been asking myself all along, but this evening formed clearer than ever. Who was Ryder but a mere mortal? It was clear he could stand on sacred ground, so why didn't he take the relic? What was so special about me? Zekiel hadn't given me an answer. I suspected Hada knew, but she wouldn't provide answers without bargaining.

I did not muse long as I ran, for the rough terrain quickly left me gasping for breath. I slowed my pace until I saw the bodies, nothing but prone shapes in the darkness. Unable to tell whether they were alive or dead, I continued my pace until the scattering of rock and dirt forced me to walk. Picking my way through the destruction, I aimed for the light, aware the night was dark. I had little time before the town would be roused and help would arrive.

A hound dashed at me, growling, and even in the duskiness, its sharp teeth were clear to see. I clasped my hands over my mouth, trying to keep from crying out as I backed away. Just as I turned to flee, an arrow flew by me and sank into its neck. It collapsed, legs twitching, and my stomach rolled with both relief and nausea.

This was the work of Zekiel. He stood at the bottom of the hill, keeping me safe even though he could not walk on this ground. I'd suspected he had other abilities or enhancements that humans did not possess. With the flight of the arrow and how quickly it had reached its target, I guessed he must have keen eyesight or even the ability to see in the dark. It made sense for the king of a midnight kingdom.

I reached the hilltop without another incident, although around me lay bodies. I tried not to look, anticipating the carnage of broken bones and smashed limbs. All was still. No moans came from those forms, nor could I hear drums anymore.

A sense of uneasiness washed over me as light bloomed on my face, a radiance similar to the light of the moon, only smaller as it glowed under stones. I shifted them as quickly as I dared, and it wasn't long before wetness dripped down my cheeks.

I was crying.

Tears streamed, and I wasn't sure if they were for myself or those who'd died so Zekiel could have another precious relic.

Broken stones dug into my legs despite the leathers as I climbed through the rubble. It shifted under my weight, and the white light glimmered brighter. Just a few more feet. My fingers reached, and a warm buzz burst from it.

Peace filled me, burning away my anxiety.

Opening the bag, I pulled out the gem, a similar shape to the moonstone, although the light wasn't as bright nor as pure. Side by side, it was easy to tell the difference.

The moonstone was wedged between two stones, and it took some yanking before I freed it. I held it up in both hands, a sense of dark glee coming over me. I'd done it! Quickly, I put the lesser gem in its place as voices rang out.

"To the tower! Protect the relic!"

My elation faded into panic. Slipping the relic into my bag, I glanced behind me. Shapes moved at the rise of the hill. Without thinking, I scuttled down the other side, keeping low, unsure whether they'd seen me make the switch.

As soon as I was free of the rubble, I ran toward the trees, cursing as I realized instead of going back the way I'd come, I'd gone down the opposite side of the hill, away from Zekiel.

The short barks of a hound echoed in the eerie night, reminding me of my escape from the Queen's guard and my flight into the shadowy forest. Blood rushed through my ears as I quickened my pace and dashed into the false safety of the wood.

Shouts rang above me as I came to a stop and

pressed my back against a tree trunk. Had anyone seen me?

I peeked back at the hill, listening to indistinguishable words, and then the light went out. They must have found the substituted gem. Would they know it was a fake?

Flattening my back against a tree, I waited for my eyes to adjust to the dim light, searching for the shimmer of Zekiel's hair. I saw nothing. As I'd suspected, I'd gone the wrong way. I worried my lower lip between my teeth as I determined what to do. This task was important to Zekiel; he'd find me, one way or another.

Yet another thought snaked through my mind: while my actions had been an accident, it also presented me with the opportunity to escape. I clenched my hands into fists, trying to embolden myself. Surely, it would be easy to slip away from the wood and start a new life. The people who lived here might take me in or allow me to find some kind of work. Zekiel hadn't explained exactly where we were, but I could only hope it was far away from my former kingdom.

The idea of leaving him left me queasy, but I'd seen his work. What he did had a dark tilt to it, a calculated coldness that did not care for life, only what he could take. I couldn't allow myself to be part of his darkness, to be ruined by his ill deeds. Stealing was a crime, but stealing sacred relics was like stealing from the gods.

What kind of fate was Zekiel playing with, and what curses and punishments would come due?

I had to leave before it got worse. I'd find the leader of this town and come forward with the relic, claiming I'd found it after the thieves brought down the tower. It wasn't a likely story and needed work, but it was all I had. Hopefully, instead of looking at me with suspicion, they'd regard me as a hero.

Sagging against the tree, I tried to work up my courage. Was I really going to do this? Leave him and his mysterious kingdom behind? There were parts of it I was coming to enjoy, budding friendships I'd never get to explore further. Besides, I didn't quite know why he needed my help, and that niggled at me.

A deep-throated murmur vibrated through the silence and then came a ragged cry. I clutched the bag with the relic to my heart, wishing I could see in the dark. The wood had been silent thus far, but I was alone in a strange land. Anything might be out there, drawn to the wreckage of the tower and the opportunity it presented.

Glowing eyes appeared like pale lamps as a beast moved toward me. A hound? No, not a hound, because it stalked toward me on silent feet. A stench filled the air, those eyes locked on me as it growled again. Heart in my throat, I took a step back, then another. Not running—for that would invoke a chase—but cautiously moving away.

Shouts ran from the hillside. "Search the wood!"

It did not deter the creature from stalking me. It growled again, pace increasing as though it were readying itself to attack. Tiny lights headed toward me: the searchers carrying lanterns. If they caught me with the relic...

Spinning around, I ran, that terrifying creature behind me. Branches whipped out, striking at me as I fled blindly into the wood. I felt the warm of breath against my legs, felt the swipe of claws across my back. Pain ripped through me, but I keep going, unwilling to stop, knowing one scream would bring the wrong people to my side. I might be saved from the beast, but they'd hang me as a thief.

The very thought made my feet move faster, until I slammed into what must have been a fallen tree branch. The air whooshed out of my body, and I lost my footing. Dizzy, I gasped for air as the creature bowled into me, knocking me flat on my back. The relic was trapped beneath me, digging into my stomach as teeth clamped down on my shoulder. I screamed because there was no hope now. The creature would eat me and when the searchers found me, it would be far too late.

Teeth broke my skin and I screamed again. How painful was being eaten alive? Tears leaked from my eyes as the pressure on my back increased. I was to be smothered, too?

Suddenly, the weight lifted. Snarls came from behind me, along with a strange hacking sound. Moments later, a voice floated out of the darkness.

"Celeste."

Zekiel.

My entire body relaxed as he flipped me over. In the darkness of the wood, it was impossible to see anything aside from the pale hues of his hair. He cradled me in his arms, and I held onto him, a sob buried deep somewhere.

"I've got you," he murmured. "You're safe now."

A burst of emotion surged through me. Relief. Anxiety. Anticipation. Hope. It was so strong that words failed me completely. Instead, I squeezed his arm, determined not to let go. With some difficulty, Zekiel placed the relic in my lap, and then he stood. My head sank against his chest and exhaustion overwhelmed me as he carried me away.

The sounds of the night faded, no more shouts or spots of light in the distance, no more hounds or strange beasts in the wood coming to attack me. I was safe. With him.

27

CELESTE

I must have passed out, for when I woke, it was still dark, but I lay in a bed. I breathed in, my scars from the forest nothing but a dull ache. Blinking, I watched the flicker of a dying fire and then, even more surprising, noticed Zekiel slumped in a chair in front of the fire. I sat up, taking in the small room. A sour note hit my belly as I glanced around me. This was nowhere I recognized, which meant…had something gone wrong?

"Zekiel?" I whispered, stumbling out of the bed.

My shoulder throbbed from where the maw of that unholy beast had bitten me, but other than a wave of exhaustion, I felt fine.

Zekiel opened his eyes, as though he'd been sleeping in that uncomfortable position, the dying light showing me they were red rimmed, his face drawn.

Still, the lines around his mouth softened as he faced me. "Celeste."

The way he said my name sent a halo of warmth through me. I rested my hand on his shoulder. "Take the bed; I'll sit here."

His arm found its way around my waist, and he drew me closer, looking up at me. "I should not sleep but keep watch. Rest while you can, for there is naught else to do."

My gaze flickered to his horns. Up close, they weren't solid black, but ridged with shades of dark gray, smokey like his eyes. I wanted to run my fingers over them but sensed the impropriety of that action. Instead, I returned to the conversation. "We haven't returned through the portal, have we?"

Zekiel frowned, his gaze drawn back to the dying embers. "No, the woods were full of them and…that beast that attacked you wasn't natural. Someone else with magic is here to halt our progress."

I shuddered. "Who else knows?"

"Many people know the ancient tales of the relics. Few have done the research to find them, and most are halted by the same problem I had. No one is worthy to walk on sacred land and take the relics."

I stared at the fall of his hair and the slump of his shoulders. The unanswered question hummed louder in my mind. *Why me?* At least Zekiel was speaking freely, and I needed to encourage him. "Will you tell me the legend while we wait?"

Those deep eyes pinned me in place, and I swallowed hard, a fluttering beginning deep in my core. We were alone and perhaps would be uninterrupted for a long while. His lips parted, and the urge to lean in and lose myself in him was so strong, I almost groaned out loud.

Zekiel's arms tightened on my waist. "Aye, sit with me."

I slid into his lap, keenly aware of every inch of his body as I settled. His grip on me tightened and his hand rested on my upper thigh, so close to the junction of my legs. I swallowed hard. Desire burned like the flames of an intense fire as I held his gaze. He felt it too, didn't he?

"It is said that in the days of old, gods walked among this world, giving gifts to mortals," Zekiel began, his fingers tracing a pattern on my back. "There are many tales of them and their interactions with our world. However, two in particular stand out to me. The one more relevant to us speaks of how the gods saw that humankind was evil. No matter what was done, people were hellbent on causing destruction and chaos.

"Heartbroken, the gods left this land to be ravaged by the whim of its inhabitants. When they forsook it, the tears they'd cried were buried in the land, creating four sacred relics. I am searching for the tears of the gods, for legend holds when one has all four, they will have power like the gods, and nothing will stand against them."

My skin tingled from his touch and the words he spoke. He sought power, just like any mortal king. "You need this power to help your kingdom," I said.

"Correct, and unlike those who have sought the relics before me, I do not seek them for selfish reasons, but to help others."

I went stiff, thinking of the bodies surrounding the tower. How was that helping others? An inkling of darkness crept into the back of my mind. "Why do you need me, specifically, to help you with this quest?"

"A fair question." Zekiel's arm around me tightened, sensing my conflict. "After the gods left the land, human and inhuman alike sought the relics. Inhumans had an advantage. We are stronger, faster, often have magic, and live much longer than mortals. Still, finding a relic often led to great calamity: many fell to their deaths, shattered into dust, or went mad. In time, it became known that inhumans could not stand on sacred ground. In fact, according to the legends, a mortal with a pure heart and of royal blood is the only one who may take the relics for themselves."

Royal blood. Understanding finally dawned, and I turned my face away, watching the dying fire. Indeed, I was a tool to be used for his purposes, yet I could not summon anger. "But I'm not keeping the relics, I'm giving them to you. Aren't you concerned about curses?"

"I will use the relics to fight evil. My motives are pure."

Biting my lower lip, I studied him, considering what Petra had said about him helping refugees. Words sprang unbidden from my lips. "You are the King of Hearts. You help others, but out here, everything is different. I saw the tower explode, saw the bodies. We aren't helping anyone here. We are taking and causing chaos to help ourselves. How will the gods see this as different?"

"A fair question indeed," Zekiel said, his voice rough. "I don't pretend to be anything that I'm not. I'm a king and I am ruthless, but I owe a responsibility to my kingdom, to my people. I cannot let them down, and anyone or anything who stands in my way will be destroyed. Don't be fooled, Celeste. What I do is not out of the kindness of my heart. I'm using you for my needs, so I can save my kingdom and take revenge on my enemies."

It was the raw note in his tone that undid me. Whatever haunted him was also destroying his peace, an emotion I knew well. I wondered if sharing with me brought him solace or only increased his agitation. I gave his shoulder a comforting squeeze as I faced him. "Zekiel, you seek to damn yourself with your words, but I'll remind you, as you've reminded me many times, that I signed the contract of my own free will. Being with you, in your kingdom, helps me too. I will admit that the enormity of what we are doing frightens me, but I will keep my word and see this through."

Zekiel groaned, resting his head against mine. "I

don't deserve that, especially after what I've shared with you."

"Because you feared I'd run away?"

"It has crossed your mind many times, hasn't it?"

I nodded, wondering if I should tell him about the fairies since we were being honest with each other.

Zekiel tilted his head, smokey gray eyes smoldering as he studied me. "I don't blame you, hence the contract. I do feel guilty for binding you to my fate. If I go down, you go down with me."

"Then we must not fail," I said firmly.

"It would be easier if I didn't care, but I find you irresistible, as if you have some hold over me, some delectable magic I wish to sink into. If time is short and my doom is sealed, then I would have you."

Such words made my heart skip. No one had spoken to me in such a way, never seen me or cared. I twisted my fingers in his shirt, pulling him to me, but there was no need.

His lips crushed against mine in an all-consuming, passionate kiss. He held it a beat and then parted the seam of my lips with his tongue. I moaned into his mouth, delightful sensations dancing through my body as his tongue swept into my mouth, desperate, hungry.

Just when I was tasting the essence of him, he pulled back, making the kiss far too short. It took me a moment to catch my breath, eyes wet as I gazed at him, completely besotted.

He traced the shape of my lips with his fingers,

sending a tingling across my skin. My entire body warmed to him, and I took a shuddering breath, not only desiring, but desperately needing more of him. I licked my lips, angling my head and leaned in, once again unable to speak aloud what I wanted, only hoping he'd read my mind, break the tension between us, and give in to our mingled desires. We hadn't finished what we started in the greenhouse, and my patience was wearing thin. I'd go wild waiting for him to take me.

The chair gave a creak as Zekiel shifted, hesitating. "There's another reason I need you, Celeste. You have a pure heart and I… I don't want to ruin you with my darkness. There's a cost to being inhuman, and while I do what is good and right most of the time, there's a vengeful, darker side to me because of my past."

"Do you think I care about your past?" I breathed, too lost in lust to care about the warning in his words.

"You should," he whispered.

"I don't," I contradicted, moving against him, my hips rocking of their own accord as I leaned in to kiss him again.

His fingers slipped beneath the waistband of my leathers as I moaned into his mouth, enjoying the feel of his rough fingers against my skin. "Zekiel," I breathed, my words lost as he trailed kisses down my neck.

Another warning creak came from the chair, but I didn't care. Arching my back, I tilted my head to give him more access. The chair gave another splintering creak and then collapsed.

Zekiel and I landed on top of splintered wood, his arms still around me. The look of astonishment that crossed his face was so enduring, I burst into laughter, then slapped a hand over my mouth to quiet my giggles. He gave me an incredulous look, lips curving up into a smile, just enough to reveal his fangs. He tugged my hand away from my mouth. “You are always lovely, even when you laugh. Don’t hide.”

I broke into a smile, the compliment warming my heart.

“I supposed the bed would be sturdier,” he said, helping me to my feet.

Alone, I retreated to the bed while Zekiel took his time tossing the broken pieces of the chair into the fire. Begrudgingly, it flickered back to life, warmth filling the room as Zekiel turned toward me. He held my gaze as he undressed.

Cloak, shirt, boots and then his pants followed until he was in all his naked glory: taut, hard muscle tapering down to the deep v of his waist, the curve of his buttocks, his thick, long cock. I couldn’t take my eyes off it as he approached. A finger hooked under my chin, and he lifted my face to his. “Is this what you want?”

“Yes.”

“You are sure?”

“Yes.”

"Lift your arms."

Wordlessly, I held up my arms and he slipped my shirt over my head, undressing me slowly, until I wore nothing more than the golden necklace with the harp pendant. He picked it up from where it lay between my breasts. "I'm honored you wear this token."

"I'm honored you care."

Tangling his fingers in my hair, he kissed me roughly, then gently laid me back on the bed.

Lacing my fingers around his neck, I felt the warmth of his body, his weight against me, and nothing else mattered but that moment. I pressed my lips against his jaw line, then moved down to his neck, drowning in his essence. His groans of pleasure only encouraged me, and I explored his body with my fingers and mouth, tracing the lines of his muscles with my fingers, pressing my tongue against the racing pulse of his heartbeat.

In response, his settled between my legs, lips against my neck, sucking and licking. I tilted my head back to give him more access, unable to halt the greedy groans he drew from my mouth.

Desire bolted through me as his rough fingers stoked a hard nipple, then followed with his mouth. His teeth nipped at my breasts, making me jolt, then followed with the lash of his tongue.

Arching my back, I spread my legs and he bent my knees, opening me up to him. Sitting up, he studied me, kissing the swells of my breasts, the flat of my belly, drawing more pants of arousal from me.

When his lips touched my slick heat, I cried out, and his grip on me tightened. He held my legs open and tasted me as though loving my body with his mouth was an act of worship. His tongue licked my navel to my clit, sucking, lashing, drawing out my wetness until I was on the brink of madness.

My fingers tightened around his forearms, holding onto him as if the physical act would drive us to the peak of pleasure together. I watched him, entranced by his touch, the reverent look in those deep gray eyes, his muscles as he moved over me.

When he slipped inside, I bucked up into him, suddenly uncomfortably full. He cupped my face, holding my gaze as he moved, sinking deeper, then out, gauging my reaction with each movement until the discomfort faded and pleasure took over.

Slowly, the rhythm increased from steady love-making to a frantic frenzy. I gripped his neck, hips rocking, pleasure building, until together, we broke over the edge and soared. Closing my eyes, I held onto him, and a sudden determination filled me. I'd found where I belonged and I wasn't letting go, not without a fight.

28

CELESTE

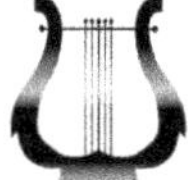

We clung to each other until the fire died out again. After dressing, we lay in bed, arms wrapped around each other, kissing, fingers lazily exploring, until a tap came on the door and Ryder burst in. He glanced at us on the bed but did not apologize or leave. Brushing his dark hair off his face, he announced, "It's clear. Best to move now while everyone is distracted."

Zekiel grip on me tightened. "Thank you, Ryder."

Ryder touched two fingers to his forehead and slipped back into the shadows. Zekiel stood, helping me to my feet as well. He opened his mouth as if to say something, then reconsidered and escorted me out.

Pale rays of dawn crept across the sky, and we moved quickly, silently, returning to the gate, which was almost invisible in the wood. As Ryder had promised, the land was quiet, only the early chirping of birds and distant howls making me shiver.

We passed through without incident back into the cool darkness of Irradiance. Zekiel still did not speak as he guided me down the scared staircase. It was only when we took the passageway toward the starlight realm that my heart sank.

After all we'd been through, even after making love, he still wanted to leave me down here. Tears of disappointment filled my eyes, but I willed them not to fall. There was a reason for this, and I had to be strong.

We returned to the chamber I knew so well, and as Zekiel opened the door, his hand landed on my wrist, drawing me back toward him. He studied me. "I've upset you."

"I'm not upset," I retorted.

He pressed his lips together, as though he didn't believe me. "I need you to be safe, Celeste. I have work above, but I will return for you soon. You did well tonight. I'm sorry to put you in harm's way; it is never my intent."

My jaw worked; there were many things I wanted to tell him, but more than anything, I wanted him to come inside and make love to me again. Unfortunately, he was a king with a duty to his people, a relic to study, a kingdom to save. I would show him that I, too, understood responsibility. "How long will you be gone?" I asked.

"A week or so, perhaps more. Yosa will ensure you have everything you need."

I nodded. "I understand that it is too dangerous above."

"It is. I will bring you a gift when I return. Anything you want as payment is yours."

I swallowed hard. That was a generous offer, but I sensed he only said it because he knew I was unhappy with the idea of being so far from him for so long.

His fingers tangled into my curls as he kissed me, slowly, tenderly, sealing the promise. When he drew away, his eyes were wet, leaving me with no doubt that he, too, felt what I felt and somehow, we were bonded together on a dark quest.

I swayed in the hammock, unable to sleep. At first, I considered our lovemaking, the tender way he'd touched me, and how I was deliciously sore between my legs. Finally, my racing thoughts turned to the legend Zekiel had shared with me. We sought the tears of the gods, and I was the one who was worthy enough to retrieve such priceless relics. How could it be?

A mere mortal with royal blood. I'd never paid much attention to my lineage, but the knowledge made me curious. Was there something special about my family line? I had stolen two of the relics without incident and felt their power vibrate through my veins, but I'd given them to Zekiel. What was he doing with them?

I thought back to his words about using me to complete the quest, that I'd be free to begin my new life afterward. Where? I wasn't sure, but the idea of leaving him was no longer tempting. Yes, I wanted freedom, but I also wanted love. Not just any love, but *his* love, despite his warning of darkness.

There was something else though, and at the time, I'd been too distracted. I felt as though he was still hiding something from me. The legend of the tears and needing a mortal princess of royal blood didn't explain everything. Next time I was above ground, I'd ask him to take me to the treasury and make a new deal with the fairies. Instead of escaping, I ask for the full truth of what was happening in Irradiance. My throat went tight at the idea of going behind his back, but my life was at risk, too. Didn't I deserve to know the truth?

Each task was more dangerous than the last, and even though he swore to protect me, events would happen that were out of his control. I'd run away because I wanted to live, yet now, I was caught in a deeper game. The seduction of pleasure should not entice me to stay, even though I was aware that in his presence, all I could think about was him. It was only alone, behind closed doors, that my muddled thoughts became clear.

When a knock sounded on my door, I almost

tripped over my feet to answer it. Yosa appeared on the other side, beaming at me as I sagged against the doorframe. "Thank goodness. Am I glad to see you. I couldn't sleep at all."

Her smile faded as she reached for me. "Not one wink? What happened to you? Let's go to the springs and wash. You look like you could do with some refreshment."

"The springs? I didn't think there were any down here," I said, letting Yosa lead me down the passageway.

Yosa linked her arm in mine. "I admit, I was distracted last time you were down here and not a very good host. Sometimes, I get too focused on the work, but yes, we do bathe. There are a few hot springs down here, cut off from the river. Bathe with caution, though. Sometimes, some of those tentacled creatures end up in the springs, which makes for a nasty surprise if one latches onto your leg."

I shivered. "Are all the springs like that?"

"Don't worry, I'll go in first and make sure it's clear."

"I appreciate that," I said, my throat dry. "I was hoping to get the chance to talk privately with you today."

Yosa sobered even more. "What's on your mind?" she said, voice full of concern. "Does it have to do with Zekiel and the work he's given you?"

I nodded once and bit my lip, suddenly feeling the

urge to weep.

"Oh, honey," she whispered. "I'm sorry."

"A beast attacked me, and the tasks aren't difficult, but they are dangerous, and I'm conflicted."

Yosa pressed her lips together. "Zekiel is a good king."

"I don't doubt it," I said morosely. Her words reminded me that she was loyal to him, and I had to be careful what I said. "What I say is not a reflection on him but on what I must do."

We arrived in a dimly lit cavern with a body of still water, steam rising from it. Yosa, wasting no time, undressed and slipped inside, walking the length of the pool before she beckoned for me to join her.

I slipped out of my leathers and scrambled down the rocks. As soon as the warm waters enveloped me, my body relaxed. I stayed near the edge, concerned about those tentacle creatures, but Yosa continued to walk back and forth, as though she couldn't keep still.

"Tell me what has you conflicted," she said. "I promise to listen without judgment."

"I could use some advice," I admitted. "What would you do in my place? Zekiel has set out to right a great wrong, but during the first task, there was an explosion that may have harmed others and this time, a tower collapsed. I don't like being part of actions that harms others, innocent or not. I feel a darkness to it, not to mention that I'm a thief. I know what I'm stealing, but I don't understand why. Perhaps that would help me."

"I see. What did Zekiel tell you about the mission?"

I shrugged. "He made a choice to save his kingdom, but from what? Why is everyone so secretive about it?"

Yosa hummed as she turned in the waters, fingers dancing over the surface as she swayed between the columns of steam. "Zekiel has an old enemy, a sorceress who has always been interested in the downfall of others. She's powerful, and her realm touches all portals, not just across kingdoms but across worlds."

My eyes went wide; this was the first I'd heard of a sorceress.

"Zekiel is also powerful, almost equally as much, and that has not sat well with the sorceress. For a long time, she sought a way to compromise this kingdom and now, she's finally found it: a way to close the portals, drain magic, and allow this kingdom to become weak so that she can take it over. Rumor has it, in the early days, the sorceress was fair and just, dealing out punishment to those who were evil, but as of late, she's become corrupt like the very ones she punished. If she takes over this kingdom, there will be nowhere for the refugees to go, and all the work Zekiel has done to keep this realm and his people safe will be undone. We will be exposed to evil. I work here in Irradiance because I love it. I have the freedom to come and go, to choose my own destiny, as do the gnomes. Under anyone else's rule, we would be slaves, forced to meet quotas and give away the wealth we find instead of sharing it amongst ourselves. That is not the way. The work you do with Zekiel prevents the sorceress from winning. Does that help?"

"A sorceress? Yes, it does help, but doing evil deeds to fight evil doesn't seem like the way to win." I clasped my hands over my mouth. I'd judged Zekiel and what he was doing, and the truth of it passed from my lips, reminding me of why I was conflicted.

"If it's the only way, it shall be done," Yosa said quietly.

The bubble in her spirit was gone, and I sensed her fear, too. What if all was lost?

"I didn't mean to spread doubt," I whispered. "I'm only afraid of what the future might bring."

"It's better you voice your concerns here," Yosa said brightly, turning back to me. "It is natural to feel this way. I wish there was something else I could say or do to help put your mind at ease."

"What you've said has been a help already."

"I'm glad to hear it. The waters, do you feel better too?"

I nodded, following Yosa as we left the pool without incident. We dressed in long gowns, loose fitting and belted around the waist, flowing freely almost to the ground. I liked the clothing of Irradiance. There was no need for laces and buttons, or the help of maids to dress oneself.

As we made our way back, I dared to ask one final

question. "Has Zekiel been married before?"

Yosa giggled and then, "You are serious. Not that I know of, but I haven't been by his side day in and day out. I've gone weeks without seeing him, so who knows if there's anyone. Why do you ask?"

My throat went dry, and I couldn't respond. Why had I brought it up when what was between us felt so fragile? Especially considering the way I'd judged him and disagreed with the way he went about his quest to save his kingdom. I wanted advice, but I also didn't, because I wanted to forget about consequences and what-ifs and sink headlong into the pleasure of him, and him alone.

Yosa took me by the arm, pulling me to a stop as she faced me, her tone serious. "It's none of my business, but since you brought it up, a word of advice. I don't pretend to know the mind of the king, nor what he does in his spare time when he's not in Irradiance. I've never seen him take a lover, but why would I? I've gone weeks without seeing him and it's none of my business. I do know that he doesn't have a wife, nor has he taken a queen since I've dwelled here. He might have a fleet of lovers who come and go, or he might be celibate. Regardless, I've come to know you as a friend. You deserve so much more than to become a discarded lover. Zekiel is kind to those who work for him, but there's another, darker side to him, ruthless and unforgiving. Remember that, no matter what choice you make, he's on the path of revenge."

29

CELESTE

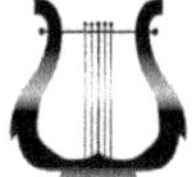

After working with the gems for a week or so, Yosa proclaimed we needed a day off and announced we were going to the crystal forest. She packed a sack of tiny crystals and led me through a maze of passageways and bridges, deeper into the starlight realm.

As we traveled, the weight of the earth pressed down on me, and the dimness of the light made it difficult to see. We passed gnomes hard at work in glistening caverns of starlight, and closed archways that shut out the light. It was so dark, Yosa had to carry a light. Occasionally, we crossed bridges spanning over ink black water, lapping against great, jutting rocks.

I shivered as we passed, getting yet another view of Irradiance. It wasn't all beautiful and filled with starlight; there were darker parts of it, too, just like Yosa had warned me about the darker parts of Zekiel. I shouldn't long to see him again, but I did. Even though I resolved to taper down those feelings, they swarmed through my mind, making the nights long and restless.

If only he hadn't kissed me like that or made love to me as though I were the only person who mattered.

At last, the scent of the air changed to something earthly and damp, and light bloomed from an archway. The ground turned from stone to soft mud, and I gasped as we stepped into a vast chamber. Crystals rose before me, as tall as ancient redwood trees, sweeping up to hidden heights of the chamber. They glowed like a rainbow in brilliant shades of pinks, oranges, blues, greens, and purples.

The ground itself glowed with wealth, as though someone had taken handfuls of gems and tossed them across the field of mud, sowing seeds. I gaped in astonishment—this shouldn't be possible. How could one grow a garden of gems? Yet, there it was in front of me, crystals in all shapes and sizes. Another look showed me that something green like grass grew among them. It couldn't be grass. Surely not in the dark, without light? Workers moved among the rows, but I wasn't sure what they were doing.

"Stunning, isn't it?" Yosa beamed, her voice full of pride.

"This is your garden? The one you nurtured from the very beginning? How did you know gems would grow?"

"Lucky guess," Yosa said. "I noticed that in all the

time I've worked here, gems are ceaseless. Despite how much work the gnomes do, it's as though they never make any progress clearing out each section. I've speculated a few times that the gems reappear in different shapes and sizes, so I experimented with growing them. These crystals are softer, but with water and limited light, they can grow as hard as diamonds. I anticipate that one day, some of the larger ones will reach the surface, which is worrisome. My next project is to discover how to take down the larger ones and carve them into something unique, much like felling old trees in a forest."

"This is incredible," I breathed, staring across the space. Indeed, it was a cross between a forest and a garden. "What are the green shoots? Surely not grass."

"No," Yosa laughed. "Grass needs light, but these are sprouts, a kind of fungi that grows underground. You'll also notice there are mushrooms too. They are responsible for some of the lights—they are translucent and reflect the light of the crystals."

"This is marvelous."

"Isn't it? Nothing like this would be possible in the mortal realm. Here, I'll take you down the paths. It can get muddy at times with all the water, so we use flat, round stones that keep our feet dry without hampering the growth."

Tiny creatures flew back and forth as we walked, and my chest went tight at the idea of fairies. "What are those?" I whispered.

"Crystal bees," Yosa explained. "Don't worry, fairies don't come down here. At least, not Hada's garden fairies. They prefer real plants as opposed to crystals."

I breathed a sigh of relief, still unwilling to share with Yosa the strange deal I'd made with Hada. It weighed on my conscious what to tell Hada when I returned above, but I couldn't help wondering how she might help me escape. Yosa's words about Zekiel being a ruthless king, hell-bent on revenge, bothered me.

It wasn't the fact that I was good or righteous. If I had become queen, I might have been forced to make difficult decisions such as the ones he made. It was only that death and darkness hummed too close to the surface, and I was afraid of the callous way he treated life. I might become part of the callous feeling, unable to give proper empathy to those around me. Especially because when I was with Zekiel, I desired nothing else but his full attention. Nothing else mattered. Was that right or wrong?

A call filtered through the air, as though it were the sound of birds, and I startled. "Do other creatures live here?"

"Only those who dwell underground," Yosa explained, stopping beside a green crystal that leaned over rather dangerously. "Something has been digging around this one. See the upturned mud? We do have burrowing creatures who find their way down here. They are pests and often make away with freshly planted crystals. The workers are placing traps to keep them away."

"It's just like a garden," I said, awe-tinging my tone. "An underground forest. Yosa, you truly have done a lovely job with all this."

"It's my passion," she said softly. "I like to see growth and progress and change. I have plans for this forest, for boats to be made of pure crystals, for statues that will decorate the castle. I imagine sculptures and furniture, even plates and forks."

I could see it too: a kingdom sparkling with crystals and gems, with untold wealth. No wonder Zekiel had enemies.

30

CELESTE

I spent days in Irradiance working with Yosa, lost in the passage of time and the luster of crystals and gem dust. One morning, a gnome delivered a scroll to Yosa, and she unfurled it, a thoughtful look on her face as she read it. "Oy, look here," she pointed, handing it to me. "We're wanted above."

Indeed, Zekiel had requested her presence above to handle a trade negotiation. He'd explicitly written that I was to come too, that he'd find me. My entire body went warm at the idea of being in his presence again. Oh, how my heart betrayed me, for in my head I'd determined to forget about him, but my very soul rejoiced at how soon I'd see him again.

I stayed quiet as Yosa and I journeyed across the lake and took the winding stairs back to the kingdom above.

Once we arrived, I promised Yosa I could find my

own way, and we separated. My original plan was to go to the hall of harps and play music to ease the longing in my soul. Instead, my footsteps led me to the patio, but this time, I knew better than to wander the garden paths. Opening the balcony doors, I stepped outside into spring.

Rolling hills and forests covered in white blossoms stretched before me. Pale pink petals danced in the breeze, and I closed my eyes, inhaling the hints of honeysuckle and cypress, a blend of sage and herbs spicing the air with a unique blend.

It was mid-afternoon, the sunlight displayed in all its glory, warming the stones beneath my feet, heating my arms in the light dress I wore. Yosa had insisted we change out of clothes covered in gem dust to make ourselves presentable. Besides, it was warmer here, and the thicker clothing we wore in Irradiance would have been too warm.

I stretched under the sunrays, almost worshipping its glory and brilliance, far different from the gemstones that shone through rock. The difference between Irradiance and the kingdom above ground was like day and night. Each had their own glory, but the light of night could, and should, never rival the light of day.

A buzzing near my ear made every muscle tense. My joy faded, leaving a sour taste in my mouth, as though I'd bitten into a lemon rind. With a sigh, I opened my eyes, not at all surprised to see Hada's rosy glow.

She grinned at me, silver wings twitching. "It's been a while since I've seen you. If I didn't know better, I'd assume you were hiding from me down in Irradiance."

I shrugged–Hada's assumption wasn't far from the truth. Zekiel had left me there, but it had been my intention to stay as long as possible to avoid her. "Surely you know my comings and goings are not up to me."

"True, but you could try harder," Hada muttered. "You're supposed to be a thief, skilled at getting in and out of places unseen."

I recalled Petra's warning about where the loyalties of the fairies lay and pressed my lips together. No need to get into a fight when I was here for other reasons. "If you must know, I'm not *that* kind of thief. My request to visit the treasury was denied, but I will ask again. I advise you to have patience."

Hada shrieked. "You advise *me*? Newcomer to this realm and *you* have advice for *me*? Why don't you visit the greenhouse again?"

I crossed my arms. "Why don't you like me Hada? Ever since I've arrived, you've been a thorn in my side. What's really going on?"

Hada sniffed. "You know nothing, and I'm sure the king has fed you lies. If you want to know what is truly happening, follow me."

I lifted my chin. "How do I know this isn't a trap?"

"I suppose you'll have to trust me." With a tug on

one of my curls, she zipped back inside and hovered in the doorway, waiting for me to decide.

Clasping my fingers together, I stared across the land, watching the glimmer in the grass that must be gems. Hada had a point. Zekiel had told me little about his kingdom, and I knew there was more he was sheltering me from. Even though she wasn't to be trusted, she was willing to share information for nothing in return. My curiosity peaked, I spun around.

She grinned. "I knew you'd come."

Ignoring the warning in my soul, I followed her into the castle.

Hada moved fast, zipping down the halls and twisting through passageways until I was completely lost. The longer we walked, the darker it became, and the air grew dense and musky. Pale lanterns lit the way, and I took one off its perch on the wall, feeling better once I had a pool of light surrounding me. My pulse hammered as I remembered the menacing growl I'd heard once or twice, as though a beast were loose in the castle. Today, I heard nothing other than the whir of Hada's wings.

A curving staircase led down, descending into a pit of blackness, and my courage began to fray.

Something was wrong.

I sensed it all around me, making the hairs on my skin stand up straight. My heart thudded like a drum in my ears, and I wanted to go back, but Hada daringly went on.

When we reached the bottom of the stairs, a foul odor filled the air, making me press my sleeve over my nose. "What is that?" I whispered, half afraid of speaking.

"Just down that way," Hada pointed to a black hole, an unlit passageway. "There's where Zekiel's secret is. The truth will help you understand that time is of the essence."

I held up the lantern but the light, instead of growing brighter, faded and dimmed. Behind me came the sound of wings, and I spun around just in time to catch Hada's rosy glow as she darted up the stairs, leaving me alone in some unholy hole in the ground.

Swallowing hard, I backed away until my feet were against the stairs. My body trembled at the idea of going into that black hole. It would be wise to flee, but I'd come this far for the truth, a truth Zekiel would not share. To protect me or someone else?

Taking a deep breath, I clutched the harp necklace, somehow resolved as I felt the jewelry in my hands. I took a step, holding up the lantern, then another and another.

Darkness engulfed me, something deeper and darker than night itself. A foulness permeated the air, and from somewhere close, I heard a guttural breath and felt a presence. Someone was there in the dark with me, but the light faded little by little. Pale orbs glowed in the dark, and a creature made of shadows moved toward me.

I glimpsed claws, limbs shrouded in darkness, horns, and a tail. A growl sounded as those eyes penetrated mine, and a ripple of fear shattered my courage. My hand shook so badly, I dropped the lantern, and the beast growled.

Blackness filled my vision, yet I could see. My skin went clammy as a bone-deep coldness washed over me, so intense my throat went dry, but my eyes were wet. I stared at the thing behind iron bars, aware that every fiber of my being was trembling uncontrollably.

This was no person, no human, or even what could possibly be classified as a monster. It was pure hatred and evil. I felt its malice crawl over my skin, its hatred for me consume me, sucking away my vitality.

Pressing my hands to my chest, I wheezed in an attempt to draw breath, only to have it sucked out of me as those claws reached, and that tail whipped. It was locked behind iron bars, so how did it affect me?

I rasped, panic clawing up my throat. Despite my efforts, I sucked in no air. It was as though I was drowning in a dungeon of darkness. I sank to my knees as a foul voice sank through my thoughts.

"Die, human. Give me your soul."

The voice was dark, layered with many voices.

My eyes burned and my body convulsed.

This was what Zekiel was saving me from: Death by a true monster. In comparison, he was a savior, and Hada, that treacherous fairy, had led me to my doom.

31

CELESTE

Somewhere beyond my dying body, the enchanting strands of harp music filled my ears. I lay prostrated, giving into my final thoughts, a collusion of madness as a spot of light filled my vision, chasing away the bottomless depths of darkness. My closed throat opened, and precious breath filled my body. I gasped, nearly choking on life-saving air itself.

Tears ran down my cheeks as I sat up, pressing a hand to my heart. It hurt; it hurt so badly and yet felt so good. Life itself had returned to me; the music had beaten back the evilness of that monster.

As the weakness left my body, I stood tall, shrinking away from the iron bars, where the creature bellowed in rage as the harp music grew louder. When I turned around, Zekiel himself walked down the stairs, playing his harp, a look of consternation and disappointment on his face. He moved toward me, eyebrows knit together, and compared to the creature he kept behind bars, he was life and purity and goodness, a true and just king with a dark and devastating secret.

My heart caved in his presence, and as he played, motes of gold floated from the harp in the shape of musical notes. Impatiently, I brushed at my cheeks, flinging the tears of fear and rage and frustration to the ground. An intense need to escape the suffocating darkness consumed me until I couldn't stand it any longer. Contract or no contract, I couldn't be a pawn in his kingdom of darkness and fear and wealth and glory.

I bolted, my feet thumping up the stairs, racing through halls, throwing open doors to rooms as I fled, my mind screaming for me to get away, away, away. Was he the king of hell itself with monsters like that, demons spit up from the underworld to torment humans with their arcane power? *How dare he.*

Heart bursting, I broke out of the castle, thundered down the steps of the patio, and dashed down the perfect path of the garden, not toward the greenhouse, but away from the castle, toward the wood. Blood roared in my ears as I ran, and my breath came short and fast, as though I were once again running from the Queen's guard, hounds howling as they searched for me.

Only this time, I was unsure what I heard: strands of the harp, my own ragged breath, the wind in the trees?

At last, I threw myself on my knees in front of a

pool of water, drying my face with the short sleeves of my dress. I'd fled Zekiel's haunted kingdom, and while reason told me I shouldn't care, I wanted to know why.

Why the horrible monster in the dungeon? Why did he keep such a creature alive, as though it were a pet?

I recalled the night we'd had dinner. When he heard the growl, he'd said that duty called, and I'd heard the music of the harp as though it played in my dreams. Was it the magic of the harp that soothed the beast? There had to be a reason Zekiel kept it, and I recognized that my infatuation with him made it difficult to think clearly.

I was at a crossroads. Part of me wanted to give him a chance to explain, but sometimes, there's no explaining pure evil. Only a need to run, to escape before the darkness claimed me. I'd felt that inkling all along, especially as his thief, but now this?

It was Hada's intent to drive a wedge of fear between us. I hated to admit it, but her plan was working.

As I puzzled through my conflicting desire, the pool began to shimmer. The water swirled, creating a whirlpool, and then turned clear as a looking glass. *Magic*. I leaned over the water, and the face of a female peered back at me.

A crown of starlight graced her head, marking her as some kind of royalty. Her wild eyes were smudged with blackness, her crimson lips plump and perfect, the angles of her pale face as sharp as crystal.

White hair cascaded behind her as she gazed at me, a cold indifference in her raven-black eyes. When she spoke, there was a chill to her voice and a matter-of-fact quality, as though originally, she'd planned on empathizing but discovered that she couldn't be bothered. "So, you've found his secret, have you?"

"Who are you?" I demanded. "What are you talking about?"

She ran a finger from her eye down to her chin, mirroring the path my tears had taken. "You're out here, crying, when you're supposed to be in there, retrieving relics for him. It's not too hard to put two and two together. You're the princess. I know because during your last quest, I sent my beast to draw some of your blood. How fortunate you were that the King of Hearts sprang to your side so quickly, before I could lure you to my kingdom. He pretends to be so wise, so pure, yet here you are, losing your mind because of him."

I drew in a breath so sharp it hurt. "You're the sorceress."

"Obviously," she snapped, voice like diamonds, eyes narrowing into slits of blackness. "I like you, so I'm going to make you an offer. Leave his side. Leave now, and I will spare your life."

I frowned. "I don't want to get involved with whatever is happening between the two of you."

"Well, you're involved, darling. You involved yourself the moment you took the Lapis Solaris." I blanched, but she went on. "It's time for the reign of the King of Hearts to end. You've seen what I've done, haven't you?"

Fear and revulsion left me nauseous. Instead of talking to her, I should flee. Instead, I kneeled, frozen in place, every muscle coiled with tension. Even though I wasn't really in her presence, I sensed her aura of power, of domination and magic.

An evil tint licked the air, as though her very voice befouled the wood, and with each cold, hard word that passed between those painted lips, a warning raced through me.

Zekiel wasn't there to help me, though, and I needed someone to explain what was happening. "What have you done?"

She did not smirk, nor did her expression change. Only her eyes changed, a glint of power behind them. "Once, there was a portal master who fell to evil ways and ended up owing me his soul. I offered it back to him in exchange for a song, a powerful song that would summon a greater demon, a demon strong enough to break the magic of the King of Hearts. Thus, the portal master played his last song and summoned a demon to bind the King of Hearts, a demon who would suck his soul, drain his power, and end his reign. You must understand, the King of Hearts and I have a history, but it is time for him to give his power to me. By midsummer, he will be trapped in his realm, unable to use the portals while the demon sucks his soul away. You, his royal blooded princess, will be part of a failed quest. Ah, I see the defiance in your eyes, but I am ageless. I've seen it all before. You will fail and you fall, mark my words. When the end comes and the demon consumes the one you call king, you will have wished you had listened to me and taken the deal. Don't you want to escape? Don't you want to own your destiny?"

"I do." I heard myself say. "I want to be a free woman and own my destiny, but you demented royals keep getting in my way. What do I have to do to be free of you both?"

"I require nothing of you. Leave now, and you shall have peace."

Odd. "What of the curse?"

"There are no curses. Whatever deal you signed with the King of Hearts will be rendered mute shortly. It was a hopeless task, after all. Find the ancient relics called the tears of the gods, break the demon bind, and free him from me. If only he knew I wear one of the tears around my neck. You could never steal from me."

As if to confirm, the sorceress held up a skull. I scrambled backward as she lifted something out of its eye: a ball of light, glowing with a pearly luster.

She was right. I'd been sent on a fool's errand.

Fresh tears slipped down my cheeks unbidden, and my voice came out in a wail. "Why do you do this?"

"Why?" She raised her pale eyebrows, as though she'd never considered why. "I thought it obvious. He has challenged my power and that cannot be forgiven.

He must be punished, as I punish all my wayward knights. A binding to a tower, a curse that goes unbroken, unless they learn their lesson. You see, I too can be forgiving. All he needs to do is give me his kingdom, and I will take the demon away. I will let him live. A fair deal."

My nostrils flared at her words, and the sorceress lifted the skull again. "All shall be right in due time, little princess, but I warn you, my patience is waning. Go back and warn your king if you must, but I recommend running for your life. If I find out you've crossed me, my wrath shall be swift and sure, worse than any curse you could ever imagine."

With those words of warning, the whirlpool swirled, water churning white then clearing as her arcane magic faded.

I was left alone in the wood.

I sat there for a long time until my legs fell asleep.

I stood, shaking them out as I weighed what to do next. For the first time since I'd been stolen, I had full knowledge of what I faced, what Zekiel was up against. Now, I had a choice to make, to save myself or…I thought of Petra and Hinko, taking care of the castle, and Yosa and the gnomes in Irradiance. What would happen to them? I recalled the conversation I'd overheard between Ryder, Yosa, and Zekiel, about the impossibilities of the task. They were loyal to him, their king, and they would fight to their very last breath.

I was but a stranger in their wood, a pawn chosen to fulfill a purpose. Did Zekiel know the sorceress had one of the relics, that she'd played a wicked game with him?

Perhaps she was right. It was time for me to look out for myself, to make a choice instead of accepting my fate, to stand up and fight for myself, fight for what I wanted.

As I mused, a flicker of white danced in the corner of my eye. Turning, I found Zekiel standing in the wood.

32

CELESTE

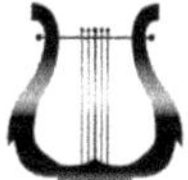

His expression was open, raw, as he approached. I balled my hands into fists, for the moment of action had come. I had a choice to make: flee his land or stay to see the carnage of his downfall. He paused, standing ever so close to me, his purple robes open, every strand of his moonlight hair perfectly in place. The faint scent of sage hovered around him, growing strong as he held his golden harp out to me.

A question filled my mind as I took it, as though it were a gift. The weight felt good in my hands, and I shifted it against my shoulder. Holding it firmly, a sudden desire overcame me, to pour all my pent-up emotion, all the words I wanted to scream, into playing.

I hesitated, recalling what had happened in my father's palace. I'd been sent to my room, scorned and labeled as odd, but that old life was gone, and I was in another kingdom, in a magical world. I brushed my fingers over the strings, and a song filled the wood.

Closing my eyes, I gave in to the sensations surrounding me. The wind dancing through the trees added a roar to my song, the sweet call of the birds adding a hint of soprano while I played the melody, letting the cry of the harp heal my broken soul. Sound belted out of me, and slowly, I became conscious of the fact that I was also singing.

The wind grew stronger, tugging at my curls, as though I were the one controlling the wind, calling forth the rain from the clouds and damning the world because I'd drawn such rotten luck. A storm of wind and rain whirled, but not a single drop touched us. We were the eye of the storm, and the whirlpool surrounded us, controlled by the music.

Power exploded through my core, and an eruption of music shattered my fear and anger. Awareness crept through me like a rising sun. It was I who invoked magic with the melody of the harp and with my voice. The storm broke, the rain ceased, and the wind soothed from a roar into a playful breeze.

Magic sprang from within me, free as it could be, and this time, no one was there to hold me back, to tell me to stop, to hamper my song in any way. It soared through the treetops, and I could see each note rising over the forest, sending pink blossoms scattering in the wind. Petals cascaded around me until I stood in a sea of pink and white, Zekiel standing with me, making no motion to brush them off his head and shoulders.

In fact, he gazed at me with the most indescribable expression on his handsome face. He'd backed away to give me space to play, but as my song ended, he sank to his knees, staring up at me as though I were a goddess who would grant him freedom.

Lightness filled me as my fingers slid off the strings. Standing shock still, I stared at him, chest heaving with exhilaration as I cradled the harp. Awe filled my soul, my breath slowing from the momentousness of what I'd done.

Something beautiful had happened, and freedom had taken root within. Staring into the unknown, I had no fear, only the knowledge that whatever obstacles I faced, I would overcome.

Zekiel, the King of Hearts, kneeled before me, eyes bright. Reverent admiration filled his voice as he whispered. "You are her, aren't you?"

I blinked at the unexpected question. "Who?"

"A legend I lost faith in. Ironic as it is, I believe in the tears of the gods, but not in the Sorceress of Music, one who calls power to her side by singing and playing an instrument. It is rare, and while I've heard of the Sorcerer of Music—an immortal who makes plants grow with his song and unleashes untold power with his music of the night—it is the Sorceress of Music who will play the melody of midnight and change worlds with her power."

Heart in my throat, I stared at him. From this angle, he was vulnerable and even more startlingly handsome. Light shone on his horns, and his light lashes were long, leaving a faint ache inside me. How I wished I had the power to take away his pain, with a word, a touch, a kiss. Still, the longing could not touch the buoyancy, the lightness, from playing. How could I feel so confident, so untouchable?

"How can you be sure it is me? This is the first time you've heard me sing and play. I can't deny I felt a power inside me, but what if it was only for this moment?"

"I've watched you," Zekiel explained. "I found it odd that your father was not fond of you playing music, but when you said strange things happened, that caught my attention. Often, when mortals are born with magic, it is suppressed because it is unusual, and there is no one willing to teach and instruct. Power lends itself to oddities, and those who lean in and practice it often become recluses or healers. They are either sought for their magical properties or hunted down as witches. I thought you might have magic or at least a tendency toward it, but you confirmed it when you played."

"You found me that day," I interrupted eagerly.

Zekiel stared past me, eyes glazed over. "If I tell you the truth, it will give you power over me, but I don't mind being indebted to you. You've already helped me immensely. I will find a way to nullify the contract, to free you, if that is what you would wish."

"That is unnecessary," I said sharply. "I met the sorceress, and she is despicable."

Zekiel's face went tight. "Ah, so she has grown strong enough to penetrate my realm."

My eyes flickered across the wood. We were seemingly alone, but that gave me no comfort. I lowered my voice, unsure if it helped. "It was the fairies, I'm sure of it. What were you going to say? What is the truth you have for me?"

Zekiel's shoulders slumped as he sighed. "Celeste, you summoned me with the harp. I was in my study, looking at maps, and I felt compelled to find you. There you were, telling me how out of practice you were, but whatever it was, it was enough to call me to your side."

I gaped at him in awe, my mouth moving but no words coming out. All this time, I'd seen myself as a victim, doing the best I could to overcome my circumstances, yet all my life, I'd had a unique power hidden within.

"Today, I called you from Irradiance to teach you the way of the harp, how to use it to harness your power, but you found the demon first."

"It was Hada," I started, then frowned. "Zekiel, since you are being honest with me, I must tell you, I made a mistake. When I first arrived, the contract made me angry and...I wanted to escape badly, even though you said there was no way to break it without hurting both of us. I made a deal with Hada. She'd help me escape, as long as I brought her a jewel from the treasury."

Zekiel fixed me with his dark eyes. "You forget one thing, Celeste. I would not still be king if I did not suspect treachery from every corner. Is this what you want, then, to complete your deal with Hada?"

I shook my head firmly. "I changed my mind after the first task, but she suspected and continued with veiled threats. Today was the final blow. She sensed I would not help her and tried to break me once and for all."

"And?" Zekiel whispered, drawing out the rest of my confession.

"I saw that terrible, terrible creature in the dungeon. Zekiel, it still frightens me, even though I know why it is there. The sorceress said she blackmailed a portal master to sic that demon on you. How could I leave you now, knowing what she did? It is just as unfair as what was done to me."

"It is indeed, but she explained all of that to you, I'm sure."

I stepped closer to him, resting my hand on his shoulder. "She was the one who changed my mind. If she hadn't appeared, I would have run far from this place. She was cold and unapologetic, as though she had the right to ruin lives and take away your kingdom."

Zekiel leaned into my touch. "She used to be fair

and just with her punishments, cursing corrupt knights and binding them to towers, trapping them in one realm for eternity. Now, she is the corrupt one."

I nodded, my confidence surging. "Only someone evil would send a demon to plague you. She should be bound to a tower, trapped in one realm for eternity."

Zekiel's eyes flashed and he stood. Gently, he took the harp from me with his gloved hand, while the other stole around my waist, drawing me against him. I tilted my head back, eyes hooded as a cascade of lust and longing poured over me. Just his touch was my undoing. My desire for him should have faded in the face of what I'd learned, but instead, the truth had set me free, and my feelings for him had grown stronger. Boldly, I placed one hand on his bare chest and gazed up at him, my lips already longing for his caress.

He leaned closer, his woodsy scent enveloping me as he whispered. "You could end this once and for all. I will teach you the melody of midnight, and then we will take her down."

The statement was bold, but I expected nothing less from a king. "That will destroy the bond the demon has on you?"

He rested his forehead against mine. "Perhaps it will, perhaps it won't. I will need to consider how the magic works. Regardless, we will have the upper hand. So, will you stay?"

"Yes," I nodded, lost in him. I'd missed him in Irradiance, missed his touch, his kisses, his love, the way he made me feel alive, how he sent my body vibrating with longing.

He captured my mouth with a possessive, urgent kiss, and I parted my lips, welcoming him, feeling I was exactly where I was meant to be.

Before I met the sorceress, I'd intended to run away and never see him again. As I kissed him, though, I realized that despite everything, we were bound on a journey, as though all along, our fates had been set to intertwine, mine with his, his with mine.

Holding me firmly, he backed me against a tree, the harp hitting the ground as a fury of passion overtook us. I tangled my fingers in his hair while he trailed kisses down my neck, one hand tugging up my skirts, baring me to him.

"Celeste," he moaned, lifting me up until I gazed down at his shining head.

I lifted a finger, suddenly daring to trace the length of his horns. He closed his eyes, warm breath against my bare shoulder as he breathed in my essence.

Hooking my legs over his arms, he slipped a finger beneath my skirts, claws skimming the curve of my bottom, the rough pads of his fingers opening me to his caress.

I was already wet, ready for him as he slipped a finger inside. "You're so tight, so wet," he whispered. "Even after all that has happened, this is still what you want?"

"Yes," I breathed into his ear. "I want you, Zekiel. Only you."

He claimed my mouth with his, then thrust inside me, his motions quick, hard, needing me, claiming me. My back scrapped against tree bark as my fingers dug into his bare bark, driving him on, craving this quick, intense pleasure.

The forest was quiet, holding its breath in the wake of our frantic lovemaking, two lovers reunited, standing together in clarity and truth.

We came together, shaking and holding each other. Zekiel pressed a quick kiss to the corner of my mouth, one to my cheek, and another to my forehead. "I don't think I could let you go, even if you wanted me to."

He released me from the tree, and as I repositioned my dress, he picked up the harp. "I want to show you something. It's also a place where we can speak freely."

"Lead on," I encouraged, my knees weak from him.

33

CELESTE

The trees opened—rather begrudgingly—around a small hut in a clearing. Moss green vines as thick as my arms twisted around the walls and bloomed on the rooftop, creating an enchanting hedge of yellow and red flowers. Tiny creatures danced from petal to petal, and my chest went tight, only to relax when I realized they were butterflies, not fairies.

Rolling back my shoulders, I glanced at Zekiel, curious as to why he'd brought me here, wondering what else he would tell me. My fingers tingled both at his touch and at the idea of using my magic again. It sizzled inside like an ever-burning ball of light, begging to be used and leaving me giddy, almost dizzy, with excitement.

"This is my workshop," Zekiel said, opening the door.

The scent of wood filled the air, reminding me of my

first visit to a woodcarver's shop. I'd been five or six at the time, and shy. I'd hidden behind my mother's skirts, staring at the woodcarvings curled on the floor until finally, unable to help myself, I stepped out and picked one up, enchanted by the way the sawdust drifted off it like fairy dust.

The woodcarver, noticing my interest, had gifted me with a tiny wooden horse, small enough to fit in the palm of my hand. I'd held it so tight the entire way home, it left indentions in my palm. It was the first gift I recalled being given, and even though I lost it a few years later, I still remembered it fondly.

Now, as I stood in Zekiel's workshop, I clasped my hands together at the sight of wood shavings scattered across the floor. I stepped further inside, admiring the blocks of wood on a table, which displayed the stages of creation, some carved and others still in their raw form. Daylight cascaded, warm and bright, on the worktable from the glass rooftop. When I lifted my face to it, yellow petals flickered overhead, giving me a view of tree blossoms and a brief glimpse of blue sky.

I lingered in the doorway of a second room, which was darker, but the natural light allowed me to see more harps in various stages. These were hollowed out and waiting for strings to breathe life into them. Just like Zekiel's hall of harps, they were all shapes and sizes, some small enough to carry, others requiring a team to move them out of the workshop and into his castle. My fingers twitched with the desire to play again and allow that buoyant burst of power to swell out of me.

Zekiel leaned against the closed door, watching me. I took a shaky breath, forcing down my anticipation, and studied him with fresh eyes. Knowing what I knew about him should have made me run. Instead, I wanted to fall into his arms, soak up his knowledge, and understand why my magic had chosen this moment to bloom.

"You're looking at me as though I've granted you your heart's desire."

"Perhaps you have," I said, gathering my skirts in my fingers.

Zekiel's gaze drifted down my body and, even though we'd just made love in the wood, a lustful look poured over his face. He swallowed so hard, I saw the muscles of his neck contract. He glided across the room to where rough-cut pieces of wood leaned against the wall. "I brought you here, Celeste, to make you a harp."

I stared at his back, unable to keep my voice from cracking as I spoke. "You would do that?"

"I owe you," he said, voice low. "You haven't asked for anything, so I will give you the greatest gift. You've shown me who you are and what kind of magic you possess. It will only become stronger with the right harp made from the right wood."

I moved across the room to him, some inkling, some longing, making me want to stay by his side. "How do I find the right wood?"

Zekiel held at his hand, palm up, and waited for me to place mine on top of his before he continued. “Each block of wood comes from a different tree, for all trees have a unique voice. A harp made from an oak tree will not sing the same as one made from a cedar tree, or an ash tree. The wood will choose you. All you need to do is feel, listen, and let your senses take over.”

He guided my palm against the flat of the wood. “Close your eyes. Let the sensations of the wood rush through you. Think of the proud tree it once was, roots growing deep in the earth, branches extending to the sky, leaves flourishing under the warmth of sunlight. Think of life and let the music well up within you.”

My eyelids fluttered shut to the sing-song melody of his tone, and I gave in to the sensation of smell and touch. Wood filled my nose, along with the scents of the forest, that deep awareness of life and growth while I searched for the music. As I gave in to my senses, I became aware of how close Zekiel stood to me, the heat of his hand over mine, the rush of my blood warming to him. The only music inside me was the song of my heart.

Blood roared in my ears as a new awareness washed over me. I felt not the wood, but him: the slow stagger of his heartbeat, his ragged breath, and a pulse of something else. A ball of light was within him, pure and beautiful, yet surrounded by shadows, trying to snuff out the light.

My skin prickled with cold, with the sudden awareness that time was short. My eyelids fluttered open, and I spun to face him, breaking the connection.

We stood so close, my breasts grazed his chest, but he did not step back. Eyes narrowed, nostrils flaring, he studied me. My lips parted to tell him what I saw, to explain the urgency I sensed, but he crushed his lips against mine.

His arms circled my waist and pressed me tightly against my body until I was molded to his. I sighed, my fingers wrapped around the taut muscles of his arms. Angling my head, I responded to his kiss, our tongues twisting, dancing, lips parting, then meeting again. Abandoning all reason, I drank him in, heart pounding, body aching for more than just a kiss, more than just the strength and security of his arms, the hardness of his body against mine. I wanted his heat, his weight, his caress, his lust, his longing. I wanted his fury, his magic, and his love.

Love. The awareness of my need made me freeze, and I broke the kiss, leaning back to meet his questioning gaze. Those gray eyes were pools of desire, and he pressed his hand against my cheek. "I lost myself," he explained.

"Don't apologize. I want you as much as you want me, but we should talk."

"That is the other reason I brought you here," he whispered, lips brushing my forehead.

I drew in a deep breath, inhaling hints of cypress. My legs parted instinctively, and it took all my willpower to regain my self-control. "When I touched the wood, I sensed life, and then I felt you. Time is short, isn't it?"

Zekiel's arm tightened. "It is. Soon, my magic will weaken, and I'll no longer be able to protect this realm. I'll no longer be king."

Those words hurt like a dagger to the heart. "Because of the demon."

"Aye."

"But you have me. I'm here to help. You have two of the tears…"

"That's what I wanted to talk to you about, but come, sit down. I sense no one has shared this knowledge with you."

He pulled out two chairs and we sat across from each other, so close our knees touched. Zekiel took my hands in his, and I closed my fingers around his gloved hand, willing myself not to flinch away from his touch. His hand felt normal, leaving me mystified as to why he kept it covered.

"Celeste, do you know who you are?"

I swallowed hard, startled by the question. "You know who I am. It's written on the contract. Princess Celeste of Domingo."

"And, I suspect, the only living heir of your parents, the only true royal left."

I blinked back tears at their memory. "Zekiel, you're frightening me. What's going on?"

"This queen you ran from, I believe she was sent to

the kingdom on purpose, with a mission to kill off first the king, and then you. She failed, and you escaped."

"But why? I know my father had enemies but. . ."

"I'm sorry Celeste, but this time, it had nothing to do with you, and everything to do with me." I stared at him, my heart beating harder. "It's because of your bloodline. You're one of the ancients, a direct descendant of the very first human, and your bloodline is still pure."

I opened my mouth, but no words came out.

"Ancients are legendary. Mortals don't speak of them, often because what they know has faded into legend. Ancients are mortals with magic, with the potential for great power. Many still exist with power in their blood. They often find they are adept at many things, skilled or more talented than others. This causes envy, and many of them hide in long-forgotten places, where oddities are natural. Often, you'll hear stories of witches, of impossible things happening, stories that sound like fables, of a time when the world was young with magic and power and possibilities."

"You think...You believe I'm an ancient?" I gasped.

"I know you are. The day you signed the contract, you signed with your blood, and as I told you, blood does not lie."

"You've known all along, and you never told me?" I squeaked.

"That's why I left you in Irradiance, to keep you safe. I couldn't take any chances that the sorceress should discover her plot failed, that I had you with me after all."

I rocked back and forth in the chair, stunned, more questions relentlessly pressing in my mind. "What does that mean for the quests, for the tasks?"

"We go on. I swore to keep you safe, but there might be another way."

My fingers closed around my necklace, my mind reeling from the new information. "Zekiel, there must be another way. The sorceress herself carries one of the tears. She showed it me, gloating because there's no way for you to break her spell."

Zekiel's eyes went dark and a cursed left his lips. "Of course, she would toy with me this way."

For the first time since my magic had awoken, a twinge of discomfort flew through me. I stood, unable to sit any longer, and paced. "She said you had a history." I closed my eyes, unable to ask if they'd once been lovers in the past.

"I worked for her, as did many other knights," Zekiel said hoarsely. "I had a rough upbringing as an orphan, working for cruel masters. When I discovered my magic, I liberated myself, along with the other orphans, but we needed a home. The sorceress welcomed us in and sent us on quests through many worlds. We became her knights, and I was content to be a follower until I discovered Irradiance. You've seen the glow on the gnomes' faces, the luster of gems. It calls to all of us. It was there I realized I could be different from those who'd come before me. I could open my home to the lost and forgotten, the weak and downtrodden, those who needed an escape, a home. Instinctively, I knew the sorceress would not approve of my decision, so I worked in secret to create portals she knew nothing about, sealing them with magic she could not break. Many lauded me as being more powerful than the sorceress, but I was simply clever. When I announced I was leaving, she was furious, but I'd fulfilled my duties. I left and set to work, and occasionally, as other knights fulfilled their duties, they'd join me."

"All this because of jealousy?"

"When one's life becomes long and days endless, there is always a desire for more: more power, more wealth, more riches. The sorceress has been the greatest power, uncontested, for a long time, but now, my name and her name are mentioned in the same breath, and my kingdom is preferred. That is why she wishes to bring me down: for daring to leave her presence and build something for myself. It is forbidden. Other knights might become disobedient and bold, leave her services to do what I have done, so I must be destroyed as an example."

"Then what will you do?"

"We go on and find the third tear so that she cannot use that power against us, and then you will play."

I looked at the wood, a lump in my throat. "But how

will you break the demon bond if not with the tears of the gods?"

Zekiel took my hand, drawing me back to him. "I don't think I can. I've tried many ways with many songs, but you? You might be able to."

34

CELESTE

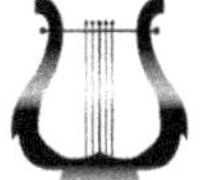

It was the wood of an ash tree that called to me, and that afternoon, Zekiel began his work. I helped as much as I could, my mind in a fog from what I'd learned. I recalled my mother, at least what I remembered of her, and my father. Perhaps he treated me the way he had because he knew the truth and was trying to protect me. I'd never know for sure. I yearned to know what my parents had known about our bloodline, and whether it was strongest on my father's side or mother's. I hadn't read about the ancients or known about magic and power. Now, I ached to sink into the knowledge and learn everything.

Zekiel told me stories as he worked, legends he'd grown up with, and I drank in his stories eagerly. In his workshop, it was easy to pretend a cloud of doom didn't hang above our heads.

When evening fell and the light faded, Zekiel stood,

brushing wood chips from his clothes. "We should return."

I glanced at the light, and it was only then that fear washed over me. To return to that haunted castle with the demon trapped underground; I recalled the way my breath had been stolen, and the tightness of my chest without air.

As though sensing my fears, Zekiel gathered me in his arms. "Stay with me tonight. I will not leave your side nor let any harm to come to you. If you sense anything dark at all, you must play, and your magic will keep the demon at bay."

"Is that what you've been doing all this time?"

"I play every night to soothe the beast and slow down its feeding, but I also play to break the bond."

I nodded as we stepped into the night. The air was cool, and I placed my hand on Zekiel's arm, staying close to him as we walked. "What does the bond do?"

"It keeps me from killing it. Whatever harm I inflict will also be inflicted upon me. When it first came, I attempted to burn it, not knowing how the magic worked." He held up his gloved hand. "I burned myself almost down to the bone."

"Oh, Zekiel. Does it still pain you?"

"Every day, except when I play. It chases away all pain."

I stared at his hand. "Let me play for you tonight."

"I'd be honored."

The wood remained silent as we walked. At last, the

castle appeared, and Zekiel opened iron gates. We passed into a courtyard, statues hulking in the darkness. Still, I held my nerve.

Lights flickered on as we passed, and Zekiel led me up curving staircases to his chamber. He pushed open double doors, revealing a circular tower with windows on three corners. It was too dark to see much of a view, only the vague shapes of bushes beneath us. A fire was lit, revealing rich carpets on the floor, elaborate paintings on the inner walls, shelves covered with books and scrolls, and a table in front of the fire. There was also a bed, a chest at the foot of it, a wardrobe on one side. If it were bright, it would have been glorious, but in the shadows of evening, it only made the encroaching doom seem real. I shivered and Zekiel touched the small of my back. "One moment," he murmured.

He placed the harp on a shelf. It surprised me to see it was the only one in the room. Going to the windows, he pulled the drapes closed and lit the candles. The halo of light eased my fears, and I stepped inside, shutting the doors behind me. Removing my slippers, I let my feet sink into the carpet, despite all we'd done together, suddenly shy that I was alone with him in his chambers.

Zekiel crossed the room, winding his arms around me he pressed my head against his chest in a loving embrace. I held onto him, listening to the thud of his heartbeat. Today, I'd finally learned the truth and felt that all barriers between us had been eliminated. All his secrets were laid bare, and I knew his weakness. It suddenly frightened me, the knowledge that if someone did sneak into the castle and slay the demon, they'd also be killing Zekiel. My grip on him tightened. How dear he'd become to me.

"You shouldn't want me," he whispered, fingers tangling in my curls.

I lifted my mouth to his ear, whispering in return. "I could say the same thing to you."

A gentle rap on the door interrupted us, and reluctantly, he let go of me. He opened the door just enough for me to see Hinko on the other side, carrying a tray. "I have a guest tonight," Zekiel said. "Please bring another plate and a bottle of wine."

Leaving the door cracked, he turned back to me with the tray. "Have you eaten today?"

"I can't say I've found myself hungry," I admitted.

He gave me a half smile. "I imagine not."

He placed the tray on the table and with a bow, he pulled out a chair. "My lady."

Hinko returned shortly with another tray, a bottle of wine, and two glasses. Although the food was delicious, it only delayed the inevitable.

I ate little, taking a few sips of wine, studying Zekiel when he wasn't studying me. The weight of where I was settled heavily on my shoulders. I was in his chambers for safety, but I wanted more than a night in his bed, yet the words would not come to me.

"Let me play for you," I said when I finished.

Without waiting for a response, I stood and retrieved the harp. Settling myself on the chest, I plucked a few strings, then closed my eyes and played whatever melody came to me. No words went with this song, only a hopeful melody translating the cry of my heart, my desire for him, into an enchanting melody.

I felt his presence beside me, but I did not open my eyes. I let the music play as his fingers grazed my cheeks, ever so slowly and gently. My skin tingled under his touch as he traced a line down the column of my neck, planting kisses where his fingers touched.

Placing both hands on my shoulders, he pressed me against his chest with a sigh, then exposed one shoulder, barring it to his caress. His lips against my bare skin sent delicious shivers up my spine and again, I felt that ache between my legs. My nipples went hard, and tension coiled as my body begged to be touched, to be taken by this king. Again and again.

His thumb brushed my chin, tilting my head up, and then he kissed me, consuming me. Opening my eyes, I let go of the harp and wrapped my arms around his neck. He skillfully moved the harp away and lifted me in his arms, placing me on the bed. Shrugging out of his royal robe, he joined me, and I sucked in a deep breath at the sight of him half-naked. Reverently, I traced my fingers down his shoulders, feeling his hard muscles, my pulse throbbing as I imagined being pressed up against him again. He kissed me again, claiming, taking, and I parted my lips, welcoming him in.

We kissed in a tangle of limbs, grasping fingers, twisted tongues, greedy lips. We kissed until we were both panting, but it was Zekiel who rose on his elbow, one hand cradling my cheek. His stormy eyes were pools of desire, and his nostrils flared as he caught his breath. "You will be my undoing," he said.

I pressed my palm to his heart. "I've come to save you, not ruin you."

"I know, and instead of letting you help, I want to whisk you somewhere safe, away from this madness, but that's not what I meant. My heart has always been cold and closed away. You make me want to be a different man. You make me want to live a life of love. This gentling within, this desperate need, is something I have never felt before. I can't go back to the way life was before you came, and it's not because of your magic. I've known about your blood for a long time. I didn't expect to care, and I tried to stay away, but I'm falling headlong and it's the most delicious, exquisite feeling I've ever felt. It's better than the sweetest wines, the most beautiful gems. I want to wrap you in the fine silks, cover you in diamonds, and make love to you over and over again."

My heart throbbed, bursting, leaping with joy. "Such poetry from your lips, my king," I whispered. "I played my heart, but you speak yours. Was there ever any doubt? I'm yours."

"You need to be certain before making such a claim."

"I am. Today has brought clarity and certainty I've never experienced before. I'm no longer lost and alone. I have a new home and a purpose. You, Zekiel, have a bold quest, and I admire what you've done here. I want to help you."

His eyes glistened, and he took my hands, kissing my knuckles. "Will you be my queen?"

"Yes," I breathed. "Yes, Zekiel, I will be your queen."

35

CELESTE

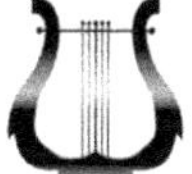

The flickering flames cast Zekiel's shadow on the wall, displaying a horned figure leaning over the bed. "I've dreamed of this," he murmured.

My heart thrummed in my chest and my entire body burned with a dizzying array of sensations.

Had I heard right? He asked me to be his queen.

"Zekiel." I broke off and licked my lips, that ache between my legs making me shift, wanting, needing him to fill me completely.

Zekiel glanced at me out of lidded eyes. "No more questions. Let me pleasure you."

Then, he lifted his hand and extended his claws.

I watched, my heart skipping as those wicked sharp edges extended, sharp as knives. I'd seen what he'd done with his claws, how he could rip and shred, and yet he brought them so close to my smooth skin, I had no choice but to lie still and trust him.

Something cool touched my nipple and I let out a soft sigh as my chest went tight.

Using his claws, he circled first one nipple and then the other, making me catch my breath and gasp. He was careful, oh so careful, and never nicked me once.

Taking back his claw, he bared his fangs, then, using his tongue, sucked first one then the other until I arched my back, heels digging into the bed.

"I…I can't…Zekiel," I gasped.

Dark gray eyes held mine before he slid lower down my body, trailing kisses from my breasts to my navel. It was only when he hooked my legs over his shoulders that I drew a shuddering breath, a burst of awareness flooding me.

He looked into my secret place, into the very heart of my core. "You are so wet," he said.

I was too far gone to feel any kind of embarrassment. I wanted him to see that I was wet for him and ready, ready to be taken by him once again.

Yet he waited, holding me on edge, drawing out the delicious, tantalizing ache of waiting and wanting.

Spreading my legs wider, he traced a finger down my inner thigh, making my hips jerk up until I was desperate for him to touch me.

When at last his fingertips grazed my clit, a moan burst from my lips and I clenched, then bucked my hips up, hoping to increase that pleasurable movement.

Lifting his finger, he blew over my heated core, and a wave of pleasure started to unfurl, then stopped when he waited, holding me at the edge, but not allowing me to tip over.

Finally, after one excruciating minute, he returned his caress, except this time, he spread me wide and slipped a finger inside, gently probing, studying my face. All too soon, he retreated, replacing his finger with his mouth as my hips jerked around him.

He held me down and used his tongue to lick me until I was floating in a pool of euphoria.

This, *this* was what I'd been missing.

He sucked gently on my clit, then alternated between licking and sucking until my legs trembled and a cascade of ecstasy poured over me.

This time, when the wave of pleasure hit its peak, I went over the edge, a cry on my lips as I bucked underneath him. Zekiel held on, hands under my bottom, squeezing as I rode out my orgasm and then collapsed.

"I want you to ride me," he said, breath feathering my ear as he rolled onto his back, pulling me on top of him.

Gripping his length in one hand, I stroked it, up and down, eyes lidded as I watched the full effect of the power I had over him. His cock twitched in my hands, one hand gripping my bottom as he groaned. "Celeste, don't stop."

But I wanted to feel him inside me.

I mounted him and he took me with one deep thrust, then another, and another. Leaning over him, I held onto his shoulders, my nipples grazing his chest.

Another climax built, rolling as I arched against him, breathing, panting feeling his lips against my skin, his tongue in my mouth, his groans of intense passion.

We held onto each other and when our gazes met, he cupped my cheek with his hand, keeping my eyes pinned to his. It was then, at the apex of the moment I felt something much deeper, a union, a bond between the two of us that needed no words. A whisper came to my mind. *I love you*. And I knew he could hear it too, without speaking aloud.

36

CELESTE

The soft silk of my royal plum dress swirled around my legs as I strode into the hall of harps, a sense of desperation accenting my movements. Last night with Zekiel had been heaven itself, and the very idea of losing him to that foul sorceress made me shaky with desperation. If she won...no, I wouldn't think of doom. I'd focus on what I could do to ensure my future.

Finally, my title of princess and my birth into a royal family served a purpose. I hadn't considered what it meant to belong to an ancient bloodline, but it made my heart swell with respect for where I'd come from and what I'd do to honor those who'd come before me. The sorceress aimed to take everything from me, which meant I had to break the demon bond with music before she discovered I'd stayed.

I walked through the harps, stopping to touch each

one. My fingertips brushed smooth wood, and I flattened my palms over the ridges of the gilded harps, sensing, as I had in Zekiel's workshop, waiting to connect to one. Making a harp took an extraordinary amount of time, and Zekiel was careful and patient, which made his work slow.

After last night, I'd made up my mind. He'd made a harp out of ash wood before; all I needed to do was find it. Once I found it, I'd play a melody that would break the bond between Zekiel and the demon, the song he'd spent months searching for. That was only the beginning. Once the bond was broken and the demon vanquished, there was still the sorceress. . .

Suddenly, my vision swam, and the scent of earth enveloped me. I felt the wind in my branches and life surrounding me, the chipmunks digging near my roots, birds building nests for their young, vines decorating my trunk. I was home to many in the forest, ancient and old, the place they came to build and grow, for shelter and comfort. Though each season changed, life came and went, only to return again.

Just as suddenly as it had come, the vision fled and I blinked, staring at the harp in front of me. It was one of the larger ones, far too big and heavy to carry, standing almost as tall as myself. I'd hoped it would be smaller, something I could carry down to the dungeon and play. From so far away, would it be enough?

What did it matter? I didn't even know what song to play.

Gathering threads of fierce determination, I sat

down, searching for the synergy I'd felt yesterday. There, within my core, was a depth of magic, shimmering, waiting for a song to be played. I warmed up my fingers, closed my eyes, and let the melody swell from within.

There. A song flowed out of me, each note ringing true and striking clear as a bell. I played better than I'd played my entire life, a song that poured from the core of my heart. This time, it wasn't born out of frustration and anger, but of purity and truth, and most of all, love.

Somewhere, far beneath me, I heard a roar, and then a desperate growl. That menace locked far below; how could I hear it from here? I kept playing, my thoughts full of Zekiel.

It wasn't until I finished that I realized my fingers were bleeding. I'd played so long and hard, the strings had sliced the skin on my hands, and bright drops of blood pooled at the bottom of the harp. I stared, dismayed, as I caught my breath, unsure what kind of magic I'd summoned this time.

Standing to my feet, I held my hands away from my body, trying not to stain my new dress with blood. A small sound from the doorway caught my attention and I glanced up, my heart quickening at the sight of Zekiel. His eyes were stormy, his mouth set in a hard line as he gazed from my hands to the harp. "What happened?"

"I...I don't know. I was lost in the magic and this just...happened."

"All this, from playing?"

I nodded as his hands closed around my wrists. He studied my palms. "Magic is uncanny, dangerous with a mind of its own. You're new to it..."

"Yes," I interrupted before he said words I did not want to hear. "That doesn't mean I should stop. You and I both know time is short. I have to learn, to play. There is no other way."

Zekiel's face crumpled. "But not like this. Not in exchange for your lifeblood."

"It's why I'm here," I said gently. "You brought me here for a specific reason, and I signed a blood contract. Whether you like it or not, this is happening. I understand that you want to protect me, but I want to save you."

"It was easier when we had a contract and you were simply retrieving precious relics for me."

"We still have the contract."

"True. I only meant this would be much easier if I wasn't in love with you."

I stilled, holding his gaze. Last night, he'd shown me love, but today, he uttered those words, and I felt that same buoyancy in my heart as I had when my magic first broke through.

"Zekiel," I exhaled. "That's exactly why I'm doing this, because..." Heat coiled through me as I uttered the words. "I'm in love with you, and that's what drives me to succeed."

"Celeste..."

"I found the harp. It's made with the wood of an ash tree, a great tree. It speaks to me, and I must play. Unfortunately, it's too large to carry with us."

"I have a smaller harp, made of the wood of the same tree. When your hands heal. . ."

"Find it," I begged. "Let's be rid of this demon once and for all."

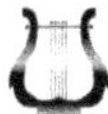

It was with great trepidation that I returned to the haunted halls beneath the castle. My hands had healed quickly, and Zekiel took me to his workshop, instructing me in the melody of midnight while he worked tirelessly. The days took on a beat of their own, fading into blended hues of light and dark. Still, I did not touch an ash-made harp until the night Zekiel deemed it was time.

He'd had the harp moved; by whom, I wasn't sure, but I guessed a group of gnomes had been summoned from Irradiance. Regardless, Zekiel carried his smaller harp, and my fingers trembled, for the hour had come to summon the magic of music and break the sorceress' foul bond.

The blackness was worse than I recalled, a sinking pit, determined to smother all inklings of life. Ignoring the creature that lurked behind gated bars, I strode to the harp, closed my eyes, and summoned my courage.

My fingers moved of their own accord, and when the first note rang out, the magic within me burned. Straightening my shoulders, I played, letting power flow through my fingers, losing myself in the melody and letting the cry of my heart be one of desire. I thought of what I wanted most: Zekiel's freedom, to be his queen, and, together, defeat the sorceress.

The sound of wind rushed through my mind, blending with the strings, and then came a guttural roar, raging against my song. I did the only thing I could do to drown it out: I opened my mouth and let a wordless song come forth. Melodies swirled, highs and lows, undulating ripples of sound.

Music transformed into raw power unfurled across the prison, and the ground beneath my feet shook. I heard a screeching sound, and a roar filled my ears. I wasn't the only one playing; Zekiel must be playing with me. Our music transformed into a command, a call to life, to freedom.

Breathless wonder overtook me, as though I were outside of myself, watching the transformation take place. Waves of music cascaded, building into a crescendo until everything around me burst. A blaze of musical notes filled the air and exploded into golden fires of light, hurling into the darkness and burning away every mote of blackness and every inkling of evil.

Blood ran down my arms as I played, slipping over the strings, but I didn't feel the pain. Eyes wide, I watched as the demon bellowed. The manacles around its arms and legs shattered while the iron bars that held it captive crumbled. The demon roared and leaped, eager to escape its prison, only to be repelled by the light.

Those blazing notes of music surrounded the demon, licking at it like eager flames. Its roars of anger turned to screams of frustration as light ate away at its body until nothing remained but smoldering ruins.

A wave of dizziness made me sway and I blinked hard, searching for Zekiel among the light. If the bond was broken, he'd be fine, but if not...a pang of horror seized me, and my blood-soaked fingers slid off the harp. My voice died in my throat as the ground gave another shudder, as though it would cave in completely.

A blaze of white filled my vision, and then Zekiel stood before me, larger than life itself. His smokey gray eyes smoldered as he cradled me in his arms and carried me up the stairs. My vision swam and my lips were dry, but I managed two words, delighted to the core of my being. "You're free."

Then exhaustion swept me away into a delicious slumber.

37

ZEKIEL

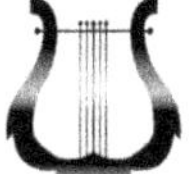

Magic was taxing and wearing, and it had almost stolen my beloved from me, but she was still alive, and I was free. I felt it with every step, a surge of power rising through me. My strength had returned, new heights of power awakened within, making my heart beat faster, heightening my senses.

Still, the battle was only half won. As soon as the sorceress discovered what had happened, she would come after us with everything she had. I only had the power of two relics to reseal my kingdom, and there was no knowing if the portals would still work, if I'd be able to come and go as I pleased.

Time stood still for me as Celeste slept. I watched the gentle rise of her chest, the sway of her curls, the peace across her face, and I wanted nothing more. It did not matter that there were maps to study, another theft to plan, letters to write, messages to send. It mattered not that a harp still waited for me to complete it, that jewels awaited trade and polishing.

She had returned my very life back to me, and it was more than gratefulness that beat within, more than admiration and respect and reverence. Part of me also knew it was more than magic, for there was only one thing greater than the power of a sorceress or the foulness of a demon. Only one thing could break that cycle of hate and revenge, and it was the one thing I'd forgotten about, the one thing I hadn't considered when I embarked on my quest for revenge.

Love. The greatest power in the universe had set me free, for only love, pure and true, had the power to break all curses. It was that truth I'd forgotten, that truth I assumed wasn't for me. I might be the King of Hearts, but I was aware my very appearance inspired dread, that the deeds I'd done were not deserving of love. Yet she came, despite what I'd done, despite my past, my appearance, even the way I'd treated her.

When she'd discovered my darkest truth, instead of fleeing, she'd stayed, despite the risk to herself. As those soft brown eyes opened, I moved to her side and took her bandaged hand. "It doesn't hurt," she whispered, squeezing my fingers to reassure me.

"It's the cost of magic," I murmured. "It demands a price. Blood itself in exchange for power. You, you've outdone yourself and done the impossible."

She gave me a sly look. "You're free, Zekiel."

"Indeed, but there's no place I'd rather be than at your side."

Celeste pressed her lips together. "You don't have to be. You're not indebted to me in any way."

"That's not the emotion I feel right now, but where words fail…" I trailed a finger down the curve of her cheek, watching the way she took a shuddering breath, her eyes flickering shut, lips parting. Leaning over her, I whispered. "Nothing has changed between us. My freedom did not take away my love for you. If anything, it strengthened it."

Her eyes opened. "Zekiel, I've never wanted to be loved for what I could do, only for being myself, and you've given me that and more. Now I know I wasn't odd. I just didn't know where I belonged."

"With me," I said, baring my teeth, a sense of protectiveness making me embrace her. "You are perfect just the way you are, and you belong here, in this kingdom. Everyone who has met you speaks highly of you, and you are free to come and go between here and Irradiance, but the future will come soon enough. I just want to be in this moment with you."

Celeste wiggled her bandaged hands. "I'm sorry I don't have my hands."

"Don't apologize. Besides," I gave her a look, "you won't need your hands for this."

She arched an eyebrow, and I kissed her silky-smooth, kissable lips, then cradled her in my arms. "Just lie here with me. Sleep, talk, rest, whatever it is you want to do. I'm here, with you, and we have no pressures, nowhere to go, and nothing to do. Let's simply be."

"I love you," she whispered.

I buried my face in her hair, breathing in her scent, almost frightened by the strength of my feelings. For her, I would damn worlds.

38

CELESTE

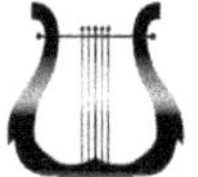

The sound of water echoed around us as we walked out of the portal into a grassy meadow. I breathed in, tasting the water in the air and smelling the scent of lemongrass and herbs. This was a verdant land, and the heat of midsummer made it even more beautiful.

For some reason, I'd thought everything would be different after Zekiel was freed from the demon. It both was and wasn't. We spent endless days together, walking the boundaries of his land, inspecting the gardens, and spending time in his workshop. He taught me the melody of midnight and continued to craft my harp. However, he wouldn't allow me to touch the ash harp, lest my fingers bleed again. The price of magic was clear. Blood.

This time, when we reached the sacred gates and the hideous specter appeared to suck Zekiel's blood, I understood her foul desire. She wished to be alive again, and by taking the blood of someone living, a few brief moments were given to her to live again, to feel something other than death. The sound of her slurping still turned my stomach, and I wished she would die once and for all, but I still grasped the knowledge of the why behind her actions.

The discovery of music and magic had awakened a different perspective within me, giving me strength I didn't know I had. I'd discovered just how deeply I'd fallen in love with Zekiel. He'd awoken my magic and the knowledge that as a descendant of the first human with ancient blood running through my veins, I was more than just a pretty face to grace a throne. With my actions, I had the power to invoke change, heal his realm, and free him.

I glanced at my king, my lover, standing tall beside me. He carried a bag and the cowl of his cloak was back, his horns on full display even though he usually hid them when we portaled to another realm. A bead of unease threaded through me, for once again, we embarked on a dangerous quest.

I still disagreed with some of Zekiel's actions; even though his need was great, it should not come at the cost of other lives. Still, the haze of fear would only lead to confusion, so I pushed it away, determined to trust him once again. "Where are we?"

Zekiel shifted the bag on his shoulder and started walking, his gait slow, as though we had all the time in the world. "We've reached the Caverns of Drysa, a riverside town close to the Drysa mountain range. The snowfall runoff provides a consistent source of water, creating waterfalls and tunnels in the mountainside, hence the canyons. They have been a source of contention between the locals and the miners brought in from neighboring vicinities. To add insult to injury, rumor has it that there's a pirate lord searching for the treasure of the tunnel: another tear of the gods."

A shiver went up my spine. "So, we are here to take it from pirates?"

Zekiel's lips curled up and his eyes flashed with amusement. "If only it were that easy. We are here during daylight because I suspect, like last time, the sorceress is aware we are hunting for the tears of the gods, and it's likely she sent agents to slow us down."

My hand went to my neck, recalling the beast who'd attacked me. "What about the harps? Will that stop them?"

Pausing, Zekiel put a hand on my shoulder. "I know you are eager to use your magic against the sorceress, but it is a last resort. You saw what happened when I used my magic. It drained me of my strength, and when you broke the demon bond, magic demanded your blood. If we must fight with magic, we will, but I'd rather use cunning and strength for this task."

"Will it be enough? Enough power to break her hold?"

"In the end, we'll have three tears, and she'll have one, I hope…"

Zekiel trailed off as he released me, and a sudden quiet came over me as we continued across the lush hillside, headed toward the gaping hole in the mountain. Scattered trees grew up on either side and at times shadows slipped between them.

We walked into the mouth of a cavern, and darkness swallowed us. Zekiel's fingers found mine, locking tight as we walked. I stayed quiet, curious why no one halted our progress. Surely, if the caverns were controlled by pirates, a pirate lord would have his guards to stop strangers from entering.

"Ryder was here," Zekiel explained as we stole around the corners. "He took care of the guards, and he's waiting for us near the temple."

"Another temple?" I asked, keeping my voice low.

"An underground one, similar to one in Viridis I imagine, but the staircase follows the path of the waterfalls and opens to the skies."

"How do you know all this? It's as if you've been here before."

"One must always spy before intruding in a sacred place. Yosa and Ryder have done their tasks admirably."

I thought of Yosa, her bright personality and passion for gems. Who would have thought she'd be caught in this madness? I understood; she was focused on saving her home, and Ryder with his stoic personality and his hawk was doing the same. I was curious about their stories, why they were so loyal to Zekiel, and what he had saved them from, but those were tales that would not be told. The past was in the past. Why dwell on it?

The sound of thunder grew louder and Zekiel's grip on me tightened as we stepped into an open space. It reminded me of the expanse of Irradiance, the cavern spiraling up, and a series of steppingstones following a waterfall to where it opened to the sky. Daylight poured down in shafts, spreading a bluish light around the cavern and the worshippers, for they didn't look like pirates. They wore blue cloaks and strode back and forth, carrying boxes and other sacks. I couldn't tell what they were sorting. Treasure, perhaps, but the area was beautiful.

Rainbows flickered around the waterfall, and drops of water fell from the top of the cavern. Moisture was everywhere, as was the bluish hue.

Zekiel bent, bringing his mouth close to my ear. "The stone steps lead up to the top of the waterfall. Careful, for they are likely slick with water. The tear is above; see the bluish light? It is said the god of water left this teardrop here, and the waters that flow here are sweet. One drop can heal any ailment and that's why the pirates have come. People will pay any price for healing water, so it is bottled and sent out from here. When you reach the top of the waterfall, take the tear that hovers there and return to me."

"What about you?"

Zekiel opened the bag and took out the harp. "I will distract them, as before."

I swallowed hard. "But the magic…"

"It is different today. A demon does not feed off me. I have the strength, thanks to you." Brushing my chin with his fingertips, he lifted my face and kissed me, slowly, tenderly, deeply.

All my hesitations faded under his touch, reminding me of what I was fighting for: him. More than him. Love. A kingdom. Freedom.

The gentle strings of the harp began, and a calm filled the air, echoed back by the sound of water. Taking a deep breath, I moved, letting the music fill me and buoy me onward. Staying close to the shadows, I slipped through the cavern while the workers turned, hands going to their sides as they moved toward the intruder.

My fingers flexed, wishing that I, too, had a harp. It seemed such a shame to keep my powers at bay.

The cool spray of the waterfall dusted my cheeks and hair with moisture as I reached the steps. Sand and stones had been scattered on them, likely to keep them from becoming too slick. I moved up them as quickly as I dared, breathing in the enchanting fragrance and considering the tales of healing waters.

My mind flickered back to Zekiel and how he'd burned his hand when he did not realize his fate was tied to that of the demon. He'd accepted it, but I wondered if it were something that could be healed. I knew it pained him still, that when I played the pain went away. It was the least I could do for him.

Ryder had done his job well, for no one interfered with my progress, and when I reached the top, a ledge opened on top of the waterfall. The cool air was a welcome change from the heat of the summer sun, and I took a moment at the top, studying my surroundings. Moss and other vegetation grew around the opening, and I imagined the mouth of the river sloped down gently from above me, creating the cascading falls. A rope hung in the water, and as I looked at it, I realized it held something suspended within the waters: the tear of the god.

I reached for it, realizing that either I'd have to use the rope to haul the relic up, or use the rope as a guide while I went into the water to retrieve it. The tear had to be fastened to something, for it was in the water but not floating away.

Yanking at the rope, I tried to free it, but it held tight, leaving me with one other choice. I undid the clasp of my cloak and let it pool at my feet. I wore a light, sleeveless dress, which would get in my way. Hesitating a moment, I slipped it over my head too, wearing only my chemise. This would take but a moment. Holding onto the rope, I swung out over the waterfall, focusing on moving fast before my fear got the better of me.

My arms strained from my weight as I moved to the middle of the waterfall, where a jutting rock gave me a reprieve. I climbed onto the slick surface, holding onto the rope with one hand, my arms shaking from taking my full weight. This was what must have been intended, for sitting on the rock, I was able to pull the glowing tear out of the water, and my breath caught. It was shaped like a teardrop, light blue from the water and shining with tiny gems. It was as beautiful as one of the treasures of Irradiance.

The tear was secured in a vase. Opening the jar, I pulled it out. Needing both my hands, I slipped it between my breasts. I reached the safety of the ledge with ease and hastily pulled on my dress again. As I reached for the cloak, I realized that I longer heard the strains of the harp underneath the roar of the waterfall.

Frowning, I spun toward the steps. Had Zekiel seen me enter the waterfall? How did he know I'd safely stolen the relic? No matter. I had to return to him. Holding the cloak, I started for the steps when a whistling sound came from above me. I tilted my head up as something dark descended from above.

A sudden fear gripped me, and I turned to flee, but that thing wrapped itself around me, arms like tentacles tightening around my lips. It squeezed my neck, and my breath turned shallow as I struggled to cry out, to sing, anything to stop this. My whole world spun, the thunder of the waterfall growing dim as blackness took me.

39

CELESTE

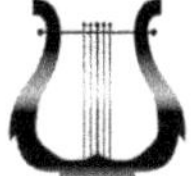

Smoke stung my nostrils and I coughed, the sound weak in the expanse. Blinking, I opened my eyes, inhaling the arid tang of incense, the potent scent covering up something much darker, dangerous.

Unnerved, I moved to sit up, but something held me back, kept me bound to a cold slab of rock. Craning my head, I made out my arms, stretched and bound above me, while my legs had been spread and bound to the stone, as if I were a sacrifice.

I'd read about human sacrifice in old history books, how in the olden days, people believed they would receive blessings from the gods by sacrificing others.

Only one person would want to catch and punish me for what I'd done.

The sorceress.

Swallowing hard, I took in my surroundings, wrinkling my nose against the smell as I tugged on my restraints. Torches flickered in the cavern, and burners full of incense smoked from the edges. Dull light glowed faintly, unable to penetrate the layers of rot, and evil that suffocated the air.

I'd been taken from a sacred place. That shouldn't have been possible, at least according to the rules Zekiel had shared. Yet, someone had done it; a human, perhaps, come to turn me in for a favor. I waited for fear to strangle me, but I felt nothing but an icy determination.

I turned my head the other way, and all sensation faded away. A gigantic white tree hovered above me, white as shards of bone, barren of all leaves, dead. Skulls covered the base of the tree, filling the places where its roots might have once been. As my gaze moved up, I understood that the tree wasn't just a tree. It was what was left of the skulls, growing into a gruesome symbol of death.

Within that tree sat a throne, and on top of it perched the sorceress. My body went cold, and a numbness sank over me. When I'd seen her reflection in the pool, I'd known she was wicked, but here, in her sanctuary, the strength of it was overwhelming.

She sat with her legs crossed, holding one of the skulls, perhaps the one with the tear inside it. Her gaze met mine and something flickered there, as though she were darkness. She was the demoness herself, taking on some kind of human-like form.

"Ah, you're awake," she said, standing suddenly.

On her feet, she was much taller than I expected, perhaps even taller than Zekiel. Oh, Zekiel. What did he think when I did not reappear?

The sorceress stepped down from her throne, her flimsy skirts swirling around her. She was almost naked, the deep v of her dress open to her navel, the slits up the side showing off her long, bare legs. She glided down the steps, but came no further, lightly tossing the skull from one hand to the next, her wicked sharp fingernails glinting in the low light.

"I did tell you to run, didn't I?" Her words were cold, with no hint of emotion. "But no, you wanted to stay with him, to free him. You're not the first one to enter my presence because of love, and I doubt you'll be the last. He is not who you think he is, and I doubt he shared the truth with you. You see, I take full responsibility for what I've done. True, I sent the demon to steal his magic, his life, so I could take his kingdom, as is my right. All my knights owe me allegiance, and he has given me nothing, after all I did for him. Who do you think allowed him to learn the melody of midnight? To have the freedom to follow his own pursuits, who chased away the hunters from his former life? What thanks do I receive? Nothing but threats. I did what I did, but he was the one who sent the infiltrator to your kingdom. Oh yes, you thought it was me, didn't you? Queen Vivian, who killed your father, the king, and made your life so miserable you became desperate and fled right into his arms. He planned it perfectly, because, you know, he has a wicked streak. Love him if you wish, or hate him, it matters not to me. I want one thing from you, and that is the tear. It must be given willingly, so I'm giving you a chance before I let my vultures rip your flesh from your bones. Pain makes people so very willing, but I'm giving you a choice, for you aren't the one I want to punish."

My mind raced as she continued to speak, tossing that skull from one hand to the other. My thoughts drowned out her chatter. One look at the orbs of her dead eyes and a flash of anger overrode my anxiety. Why the hell would I listen to the sorceress and her lies?

It was clear she only thought of herself, and her blasphemy against Zekiel was meant to turn me against him, to make me lose courage, give up and hand her the tear. She assumed I was some weak human who would fall apart because there were dark things I didn't know about the man I loved. She didn't get to tell me those things, to plant the seed of doubt, especially not here, not now. Only Zekiel could confirm those words, and I'd wait for him to do so instead of believing the vile words of a self-centered sorceress.

Blood roared in my ears as I recalled Queen Vivian, how she took and took and took. My father. My blood. My kingdom.

I remembered when I'd played in the hall for the first time, proud of my skills, until the birds had shattered glass and the court looked at me with fear and confusion. After that, others moved to the opposite side of the hall when I passed and whispered, called me odd. All those bitter memories changed when I entered Zekiel's kingdom.

No, it hadn't been my choice, but he'd made me an offer, keeping his secrets close, as any king would. Living in his kingdom had changed me, opened doors to the truth, and shown me I wasn't strange. I was important, I meant something to someone.

The sorceress kept speaking, her poisonous words trying to cut through my fog of memories. Balling my fingers into fists, yanking against my restraints, I did the only thing I could think to do. I opened my mouth. A wordless song belted out of me, cutting off the sorceress' words, as though I'd taken a sword and sliced her throat.

Closing my eyes, I sang, thinking only of Zekiel, only of the good memories. She would not scorn his name, especially not now. If I were to die at her hand, I would keep my memories. She might break my body, flay my skin from bone, but she would not break my mind. It was mine. I was in control of the thoughts I let in, and if my song could damage her in any way, it would be enough.

I sang while shouts echoed around me and footsteps

pounded the ground. Keeping my eyes closed I focused. It was the song, the song to break a curse, to combat evil. It was the melody of midnight, and I sang every note with all my might. If it was to be my last, it would be my best.

40

CELESTE

A thunderclap boomed through my song, breaking me off mid-note. The slab of rock I lay on shook, and light, impossibly golden light, blasted into the cavern with a heat that made me scream. Wind whirled and I realized the light was a portal, and out of it walked Zekiel, looking absolutely murderous.

My heart leaped when our eyes locked, and in two steps, he was by my side. Instinctively, I reached for him, forgetting my hands were bound, yet the restraints came away. Either my song or the blast from the portal had freed me. "How did you know where to find me?" I gasped.

His brow furrowed and he gave the slightest shake of his head. "I didn't. It was you who summoned me."

My mouth opened and closed like a fish. I assumed it was only possible with the harp, but magic was limitless and did not conform to my assumptions.

Zekiel handed me a bag. "This belongs to you. It always has and, I suspect, always will."

Leaving me with those cryptic words, he stepped in front of me, using his body to shield me from the sorceress. I opened the bag quickly, as I already felt waves of anger coming off the sorceress. She said something, her voice holding a dangerous note, but the items in the bag captured my full attention.

Zekiel had brought me a harp. Not just any harp. No, the one he'd specifically crafted for me. All this time, I'd wondered what was in the bag, but he'd finished the harp in secret and brought it, just in case. My heart soared as I cradled it, feeling the wood beneath my fingers, a song begging to be let out.

There was more. A faint glow caught my eye, and I opened the bag wider, chest tight as I took out the Solaris Lapis and Solaris Luna. The tears of the gods. Zekiel had given them to me. What did that mean? I had a harp, my voice, and three out of the four tears. Sitting up straight on the slab, I gathered the items around me, placed the harp in my lap, and focused.

Zekiel and the sorceress were arguing, voices loud, hard, but I didn't want to hear the words they might say, for there was only one outcome I wanted. I closed my eyes, and I played.

The air shifted around me as my fingers stroked the strings, and heat drifted from my core. I imagined myself back in Irradiance, where the twinkling lights surrounded me. It was only the crust of the under earth, where beauty still reigned. There were other places, deeper places, where monsters dwelled, forced to stay hidden, locked beneath the weight of the foul depths.

It was that deep place I searched, down in the depths, layers upon layers down, down, down, where the darkness was so thick one could feel it, and the terrors of the night were close and real. That was where the sorceress belonged, and that was where I'd send her.

The next notes I played were gathering strength, pulling from the magic within the three tears and using it like threads to wrap around the sorceress. It was then that I felt resistance. She was using her magic to combat me, fighting back against the music. I was strong, but she was stronger. I had magic, but she had unknown decades of experience, and she pulled upon all that she knew to fight me.

I warred with her, my fingers moving faster, notes turning sour as I tried to speed up, but I found myself reeling, her overpowering presence sending smoke down my throat. I coughed, my fingers stumbling, and I lost the melody. Taking a deep breath, I kept my eyes closed, trying to find my center, my peace.

Another melody filled the air, the sound lighter, brighter. I opened my eyes and Zekiel stood beside me, playing his harp. I tilted my head up, watching as he lost himself in the melody, eyes closed, shoulders straight, his fingers moving fluidly over the strings.

The magic of one was not enough; both of us needed to play, both of us needed to give everything to defeat the sorceress. Shadows leapt on the walls around me, and I sensed a crowd, perhaps her court come to watch. For a moment, I wondered why they weren't interfering, and then I realized the music added an invisible barrier, surrounding Zekiel and me, keeping them from harming us.

Finding my center, my peace, my calm, I played again, drawing on my inner strength and using the power of the tears to funnel my magic. I poured my heart into the song, playing with my soul, and the magic sprang through me, bright then strong, draining away my will, making me play as though I could not stop.

When the blood ran down my fingers, I pressed my lips together against the pain and focused on the tears of the gods. All three of them lay beside me, and when I looked at them, they started trembling, shaking, as though something was inside of them, struggling for freedom.

Ragged breaths caught in my throat and heat blazed through my fingers as those tears grew steadily brighter until one shattered.

I cried out in surprise as one by one, the sacred relics burst into pure light, golden light intertwined with moonlight, along with the sound of rushing water. Light shot out like a whip and wrapped around the sorceress, squeezing. She did not cry out. Instead, fury made her lips jerk and her eyes went so black, they turned to liquid and ran, black blood cascading down her cheeks.

"You have been seen and judged," came a voice like thunder, and the top of the cavern came off, as though a giant had ripped it.

My fingers slid off the harp and I slumped on the stone, gaping in awe as a being full of light picked up the sorceress.

"As punishment for your deeds, you shall be locked in a tower at the bottom of the sea for all eternity. Magic will never answer to you again. This shall be your curse."

The hand lifted her away, and it was then, only then, that I heard the roar of her scream, a deafening crescendo that shook what remained of the cavern.

The braziers toppled over, and then came a stampede of movement as her ruined court fled. I heard, rather than saw, the sounds of swords and fires as the court descended into madness.

My shoulders slumped and weariness came over me, so deep and intense, I thought I could close my eyes, go to sleep and never wake again.

We'd done it.

We had used magic that called down the gods and sentenced the sorceress. My mouth was too tired to smile, and the buoyancy that should have bloomed in my heart was gone. I'd played too much and too long, and the magic had taken its due.

I leaned back, ready to sleep, only to fall into Zekiel's arms. He cradled me to his chest, holding me tight. "It has been enough. Stay with me, my sorceress of music. The magic was enough. It is time to go home."

I wanted to say that I'd like that and to thank him, but tiredness overcame me. I said nothing at all as we walked into the blinding light of the portal.

41

CELESTE

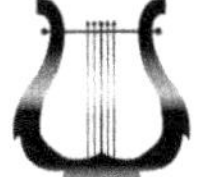

"I have something to show you." Zekiel leaned against the doorway, watching me as I finished dressing.

For the past three days, I'd slept, recovering from the magic draining me. In truth, after one day of rest, I felt much better, but Zekiel refused to let me out of bed. He brought me trays of food, scrolls to read, and played gentle tunes on his harp until I drifted to sleep, my dreams bright and full of hope.

It had been a long time since anyone fussed over me, and I was happy to let him. I glanced at myself in the mirror, my hair almost to my shoulders. I decided I liked the shorter length.

The dark plum dress I wore was rather extravagant, with a long skirt and a slit up the side, showing off my legs as I walked. I spun slowly, coming to rest in front of Zekiel as his eyes went dark, looking at me as though I were something delicious to eat.

"Where are you taking me?" I asked, voice breathy as I stepped closer to him.

Zekiel had been keeping his distance to give me time to recover, but standing close to him, I felt that fluttering within, that intense need to be with him physically, spiritually, mentally. He must have felt it too, for he drew me into his arms, where my head fit just right against his chest, just below his shoulder.

I inhaled the faint scent of cypress and smiled, my arms tightening around him as tears pricked. I would not weep, but it was hard to believe what had happened in the sorceress' lair was nothing more than a shared nightmare.

"I'm half tempted to strip you out of this dress right here," Zekiel growled in my ear.

My cheeks burned. I didn't necessarily want him to rip the beautiful dress to shreds with his claws. "I've seen nothing but the inside of this room for three days. Take me somewhere, and then make love to me."

Zekiel's slid his hands down my back, squeezing my bottom before he let go. "As you command, my lady."

Placing my hand on his arm, he escorted me down the hall. "You once asked to see the treasury, and I declined for my own reasons, unsure whether you were to be trusted."

I frowned at the reminder of Hada, unsure what I would have chosen if Zekiel had given me the jewel the fairies wanted. "You were right to wait, and I've always wondered, what did happen to the fairies? They were here for so long and then, right after I met the sorceress, they disappeared."

Zekiel grunted. "They are mischievous, and their allegiance is constantly changing. They probably went to bother some hapless fool."

"But why the ruby stone? Hada was keen, not desperate, intently curious on retrieving it."

"Ah, well, there are precious stones and relics that have significance for different species. I admit, I took the stone from the fairies in exchange for their allegiance, knowing full well who and what they were. To them, it resembles freedom or good luck."

"Interested," I murmured, and then my eyebrows lifted.

A whisper of surprise crossed my lips as we walked into the hall of harps, the flourishes of the golden instruments gleaming in the light. I glanced at Zekiel as he let go of me, but his expression gave away nothing as he strode to the largest harp, the one I'd played the first time I'd visited the hall.

Puzzled, I waited while he strummed three notes, each ringing loud and clear, echoing away in the hall. There came a moment of silence as they faded away. Then, a loud creak came, and a vault in the middle of the floor opened. Stairs led down, and the luster of light came through.

Standing in front of the trapdoor, Zekiel extended his hand to me. “Come, let me show you the treasury.”

“This was here all along?” I gasped.

I’d asked to be taken to the treasury and he’d given me the key. It was right in front of me this entire time and I’d missed it.

“Is this magic?” I asked as we descended.

“No,” Zekiel chuckled. “It’s music. Science, if you may. The hinges to the door open based on the vibrations of sound that carry through the room. I wondered if you’d discover it for yourself, and I would not have minded if you had. We are here because I owe you a bag of gems for completing the quests.”

We arrived at the bottom of the steps, and I faced him, placing my hands on his chest. “We are past that now, aren’t we? I’m staying. You don’t have to pay me for anything.”

Zekiel waved his gloved hand. “Fair is fair, and I believe you’ll change your mind when you see all this.”

Moving behind me, he placed his hands on my hips and turned me to face the front.

An enormous cavern stretched before me, much like the ones in Irradiance, except this one was overflowing with treasure. Golden coins covered the ground completely, and the brilliance of gems lit up the cavern. My jaw dropped as I took in the crystals hanging from the ceiling, goblets with every jewel imaginable spilling from them, trunks overflowing with diamonds, carvings of ivory and glass, dripping with necklaces and rings.

A golden path snaked through the treasury, displaying trees dripping with emeralds, sapphire plumes, and amethyst. The lights, the colors, were breathtaking, and I found myself walking among them, bending to touch them, letting the jewels run through my fingers.

Zekiel was right: something within me wanted this beauty, wanted this glory all to myself.

"I would have you know," Zekiel said, "as my queen, this is all yours."

I faced him, barely daring to believe his words. "But you're the King of Hearts," I stammered. "All of this belongs to you."

"And you, because you were the one who saved me."

He glided toward me, and my breath hitched as he continued. "A friend once told me that I shouldn't let revenge guide my actions, but I am king, and I assumed I knew everything. I ignored his advice, but you made it oh so difficult to ignore. I tried not to care, but from the moment I saw you in the wood, I felt something. Now, I know it was destiny bringing us together. It's been a long time since I've loved, since I've actually cared for doing more than my duty, but the sorceress broke something within me, making me desperate. You, you are more than anything I could ever imagine.

You are my destiny, my beginning and my end, the melody in my song, the life in each breath I take. You brought life back to me, and even more, you made me care again, made me feel again for more than just duty and riches. By your side, I am more. More than just a king or an inhuman or the protector of realms. I am complete and whole with you. You are the star, the song I didn't know I was searching for, and I love you, with all my heart and mind and body and soul. I would be honored if you would be my queen. I know I'm not worthy of your goodness, your purity. You called me out when I was focused on bringing death and destruction to anyone who got in my way, and that is why the tears of the gods belong to you and you alone. You were the only one who could save this realm, defeat the sorceress, and bring back the gods to enact judgment. I love you for that, for showing me that there is another path, another way to live."

My chest squeezed as I pressed my hand to his cheek, feeling the slopes of his perfect features. "Zekiel, your words make my heart leap with joy. Your willingness to be vulnerable and honest only draws me in deeper. I want nothing more than to be by your side each day. I'm honored you've chosen me. I knew, I just knew, that when the sorceress said foul things to poison my mind against you, I should not listen. For this, this is the real you, the ability to recognize what was done in the past and shift and grow and be willing to change. You are more, so much more, than anything I ever imagined. Your might, your power, your wealth... I am nothing in comparison. Are you sure you want me?"

"Don't you dare downplay yourself," Zekiel growled. "Stand tall and be confident in your power, your magic, your worth. I am curious, though; what did the sorceress say about me? What lies did she attempt to entrap you with?"

I frowned. "That you were behind what happened in the kingdom, Queen Vivian, the death of my father... that it had all been your doing to make me desperate, to lure me to the woods."

Zekiel took my hand. "I'm sorry you had to hear it from her."

My heart sank. It was true?

"I sent Hada to the mortal realm to find me a princess, one with ancient blood who I could steal away to my realm and make a deal with. I was unaware she was also working for the sorceress, nor was I aware of the elaborate scheme or the deal they made with Queen Vivian. Still, I am sorry. I am the root cause of your pain and if I'd known. . ."

"Hush!" I said sharply, blinking back tears. "The sorceress only blamed me because she wanted to drive a wedge between us, force me to hate you, but that is impossible. You did what you had to do, and so did I. What matters is where we are now. We are together and shall be for all eternity. You've awoken my magic and made me acknowledge a truth I did not realize. My parents told me nothing about my bloodline, about who I was, and what power I might possess. I was unhappy in the mortal realm, even before Queen Vivian came along and ruined my life. All that pain and sorrow was leading up to one moment, to something great, and it was the ability to be here, to help you and so many others. Tell me, Zekiel, now that you are free and your kingdom is secured again, will your people return?"

"They will." Zekiel lifted my hand to his mouth and kissed my knuckles. "They will return to see you crowned queen, and they, too, will know the extent of your generosity and kindness."

Warmth filled me, burning away all the indecision and fears that had danced through my mind. My future was clear, and I could not imagine it without Zekiel, which only left me with a fierce desire to keep him, to protect the realm, to live a life full of love, of grace, of generosity, to use the gift of magic for good.

A sudden need overcame me as he wrapped his arms around me. "The past is forgotten," I whispered. "All that's left is the future to look forward to, and I want you."

Zekiel's lips feathered across my shoulder as he slipped the sleeve of my dress down one shoulder. "Mine," he whispered, a note of possessiveness in his tone.

It left me giddy, knowing he was a jealous lover, a lover who adored me, who desired me and wanted me. Closing my eyes, I lifted my lips to his and let him take me, fingers skating across bare skin as gently he pushed the dress away, until there was nothing between us but bare skin.

He crushed his lips against mine, loving me, taking me deeper. Our tongues twisted together, thrusting, dancing until I was breathless, panting in his arms. A sense of desperation overcame me, and I pushed his royal robes away as my fingers went to the waistband of his pants.

Zekiel made a low sound in his throat, one hand twisted in my hair, his lips still pressing against mine as my fingers found his cock and tightened around it. He groaned, hips thrusting as his grip on me tightened. Then he lowered me to the floor, flinging coins as he bent over me.

I arched my back, still lip-locked in the throes of passion. Bringing my knees up, I parted them, trapping him between my legs. When Zekiel spoke, his voice was rough, raw. “I will take my time, and I will pleasure you until you know nothing else, but I need you now.”

Even before he finished speaking, he sheathed himself inside me, and I cried out at the sudden and swift burst of passion. He moved quickly, rocking his hips back and forth, taking me, claiming me, making me his own. My fingernails dug into his back as I moved with him, a desperate frenzy to our rhythm. He held me, arms wrapped tightly around my waist, eliciting moans with every touch, until I was spineless, floating on a sea of pleasure, and yet it wasn't enough. I wanted more, more of him, more of every touch. He was my addiction, and a lifetime, an eternity, with him might not be enough.

42

CELESTE

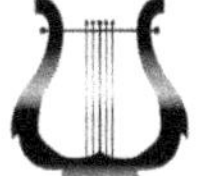

Notes of sweet peppers and fresh flowers surrounded me as Zekiel and I went down the hall for dinner. The castle was bright and airy, doors thrown open, the full fragrance of summer pouring in.

After our romp in the treasury, we were unable to keep our hands off each other. Zekiel took me again in the hall of harps and back in our room on the silk sheets. It was late afternoon when we finally dressed and headed to the dining hall. Not the smaller room where I'd initially signed the contract that changed my life, but to the grand dining hall, where I'd spent more than one afternoon having tea with Petra.

I looked forward to more afternoons having tea with her and traveling down to Irradiance to work again with Yosa. New friendships had been built, and now that I knew I was staying for good, I wanted to take the time to cultivate them.

We arrived at the doors, and Zekiel slid his arm around my side, kissing the corner of my mouth. "You look beautiful," he murmured. "Are you ready?"

I arched an eyebrow. "Thank you. You look quite handsome yourself, but what am I ready for?"

Letting go of me, he put his hands on the doors and pushed. "Ready for this."

The doors opened to the dining hall, a room I'd thought was sad, lost, and empty. Today, though, it was full of people, smiling faces, some familiar, like those of the gnomes who worked in Irradiance, and Hinko and Petra. Others were unfamiliar. There were humans, Yosa standing with Ryder, the hawk on his shoulder, and many others. There were also inhumans I guessed, because of their pointed ears. When we walked into the room, a cheer went up, goblets raised, fists pounding on the table, and they were all looking at me.

Stunned, I turned to Zekiel, but he'd stepped back to join them too, beaming at me as if I was the hero who'd saved the kingdom. Tears filled my eyes, and I pressed a hand to my heart. No one had ever looked at me with the shining admiration and gratitude they did. No one had given me the time of day or thought I was worth more than the next heir I brought into the world. Magic had changed everything.

I bowed my head and curtseyed as a thousand voices rang out. "All hail Queen Celeste."

AUTHOR'S NOTE

Thank you for enjoying *Melody of Midnight*. You might wonder what happens next, now that the sorceress is trapped. Have no fear. There are plenty of wayward knights she cursed, and endless stories to be told. Keep an eye out for the next tale: *Elegy of Twilight*.

If this is your first Tower Knights tale, and you're curious about the Sorcerer of Music, read *Music of the Night*.

If you want to know the story about the knight who called down the demon to haunt the King of Hearts, read *Song of the Dawn*.

And if you want to know more about Oren and his magical pipe, read *Lured by the Dusk*.

ALSO BY ANGELA J. FORD

Join my email list for updates, previews, giveaways, and new release notifications. Join now: www.angelajford.com/signup

Chronicles of the Four Worlds (epic fantasy)

A complete six-book epic fantasy series spanning two hundred years, featuring an epic battle between mortals and immortals.

Legend of the Nameless One Series (epic fantasy)

A complete five-book epic fantasy adventure series featuring an enchantress, a wizard, and a sarcastic dragon.

Night of the Dark Fae Trilogy (romantic epic fantasy)

A complete epic fantasy trilogy featuring a strong heroine, dark fae, orcs, goblins, dragons, antiheroes, magic, and romance.

Tales of the Enchanted Wildwood (fairy tale romance)

Adult fairy tales blending fantasy action-adventure with steamy romance. Each short story can be read as a stand-alone and features a different couple.

Tower Knights (fantasy romance)

Gothic-inspired adult steamy fantasy romance. Each novel can be read as a stand-alone and features a different couple.

Gods & Goddesses of Labraid (epic fantasy)

A complete epic fantasy duology featuring a warrior princess with a dire future who embarks on a perilous quest to regain her fallen kingdom.

Lore of Nomadia Trilogy (epic fantasy romance)

The story of an alluring nymph, a curious librarian, a renowned hunter, and a mad sorceress as they seek to save—or destroy—the empire of Nomadia.

One Winter Night (fantasy romance)

Winter-themed spicy fantasy romance. Each novel is a stand-alone and features a difference couple.

Visit angelajford.com for autographed books, exclusive book swag and book boxes.

ABOUT THE AUTHOR

Angela J. Ford is a bestselling author who writes epic fantasy and steamy fantasy romance with vivid worlds, gray characters and endings you just can't guess. She has written and published over 30 books.

Aside from writing she and her husband own The Signed Book Shop. A one-stop shop for readers to find signed books and book merchandise.

If you happen to be in Nashville, you'll most likely find her enjoying a white chocolate mocha and daydreaming about her next book.

facebook.com/angelajfordauthor
instagram.com/angelajfordbooks
amazon.com/Angela-J-Ford/e/B0052U9PZO
bookbub.com/authors/angela-j-ford
tiktok.com/@angelajfordauthor